When I  **my part... elderly w... wore a shapeless shift of floral polyester and rubber thong sandals in DayGlo pink.**

Adler made the introductions. "This is Mrs. Eagleton, the one who called us."

The woman straightened her shoulders and thrust out her scrawny chest, hiking her shift to expose knobby knees. "Captain of the Azalea Acres Neighborhood Crime Watch. I take my job seriously."

"How did you discover the body, Mrs. Eagleton?"

"I heard the howling of Precious, Edith's Siamese. I tried going in, but the doors were locked."

"That's when you called us?"

"Of course not. I wouldn't waste your valuable time unless I was sure there was a problem. I went home for my flashlight, came back, looked in the window to see if I could spot anything suspicious."

The window she'd indicated was at least six feet above the ground. "You looked in that window?"

"I used a stepladder. And my flashlight."

Azalea Acres, I thought, must be the safest neighborhood in the state. I felt a stab of compassion for Mrs. Eagleton's surviving neighbors. "Thank you. You've been very helpful."

"Is that it? This *is* a murder, isn't it?"

Charlotte Douglas

USA TODAY bestselling author Charlotte Douglas, a versatile writer who has produced over twenty-five books, including romances, suspense, Gothics and even a *Star Trek* novel, has now created a mystery series featuring Maggie Skerritt, a witty and irreverent homicide detective in a small fictional town on Florida's central west coast.

Douglas's life has been as varied as her writings. Born in North Carolina and raised in Florida, she earned her degree in English from the University of North Carolina at Chapel Hill and attended graduate school at the University of South Florida in Tampa. She has worked as an actor, a journalist and a church musician and taught English and speech at the secondary and college level for almost two decades. For several summers while newly married and still in college, she even manned a U.S. Forest Service lookout in northwest Montana with her husband.

Married to her high school sweetheart for over four decades, Douglas now writes full-time. With her husband and their two cairn terriers, she divides her year between their home on Florida's central west coast—a place not unlike Pelican Bay—and their mountaintop retreat in the Great Smokies of North Carolina.

She enjoys hearing from readers, who can contact her at charlottedouglas1@juno.com.

CHARLOTTE DOUGLAS

Pelican Bay

PELICAN BAY

copyright © 2005 Charlotte Douglas

isbn 0373880596

TheNextNovel.com

 HARLEQUIN®

PRINTED IN U.S.A.

PELICAN BAY, FLORIDA

Welcome to Pelican Bay, a picturesque little village nestled on Florida's central west coast, where the gentle waves of the Gulf of Mexico lap its sugar-sand beaches and the sun shines brightly most days of the year. The town is a mecca for tourists, retirees, snowbirds and the occasional criminal, who flock to its antique shops, upscale restaurants, boat-filled marina and the jogging and biking trails that line the waterfront and bisect the business district. As in every paradise, trouble often lurks here just below the surface. That's where Detective Maggie Skerritt comes in.

CHAPTER I

"Ma'am?"

Dave Adler, the young patrol officer with the fresh-faced good looks of a teen idol, filled the doorway to my office with his six-foot frame.

"It's Detective Skerritt, or Maggie, remember?" When he called me *ma'am*, I felt like his mother.

"Detective Skerritt." His face reddened. "We got another home invasion. Sheriff's crime-scene unit is there now, but I doubt they'll find much. It was smash, grab and gone."

I slumped in my desk chair and stared at the half-eaten burger and grease-stained container of cold, soggy fries on the blotter. Working late to catch up on my ever-increasing mountain of paperwork, I'd been too busy to eat.

"Where do they think this is, Tampa?" I swept the leftovers into the wastebasket beside my desk. "I've been with the Pelican Bay Department fifteen years and never had an armed intrusion. Now, within three weeks, we've had two. Same MO?"

Adler nodded and scratched an earlobe protruding beneath his sandy hair. "Busted in the door. But only one perp. Adult male, according to the description the old man gave us. Not teenagers like the last time."

"Anything taken?"

"A gun, .22 automatic."

"No money?" The previous home invaders had gone after cash, not bothering with anything that had to be fenced. I massaged my aching temples.

"Just the gun. Didn't seem interested in the old man's wallet, and he'd just cashed a social security check."

I smiled at Adler. The kid did his homework, and without the cocky, smart-ass attitude of many of the younger recruits. "He ignored the money? Something scare this guy off?"

He shrugged. "The victim was real rattled. His wife was in shock and couldn't talk. Maybe tomorrow when they've calmed down, you can get something useful out of them. I gotta get back on the road. Natives are restless tonight. Full moon."

I didn't see him leave. I was staring at the mountain of folders in my in-basket and feeling older by the minute. Too damned old at forty-eight. I'd put in my twenty years, and then some, but every time I thought about retiring, I wondered what the hell I'd do without the job. The pile of papers before me represented drug dealers, car thieves, convenience-store robbers and child abusers. Reentry into so-called normal society was a bigger adjustment than I was prepared to make.

I slid the top folder from the pile, pulled up a form on my ancient computer and typed the date. I typed Columbus-style, find it and land on it. One of these days, I kept promising myself, I'd sign up for a computer class at the junior college and learn to type.

I finished the first report, left my closet they called an office and walked up the narrow hallway to the front of the station. While I poured a cup of coffee with an uncanny resemblance to industrial sludge, Darcy Wilkins, the only other female on the force, was speaking into the mike at the dispatch desk.

"Contact a Mrs. Eagleton at 234 Grove Street," Darcy said. "She's concerned about her next-door neighbor. Thinks she might be ill and need assistance."

"10-4," Adler's static-laden voice replied. "Almost there now."

Darcy switched back to the telephone and assured the caller that help was on the way.

Some in Pelican Bay would claim that Darcy, an attractive young African-American, and I obtained our jobs only by the grace of affirmative action, but they would be dead wrong. We were both damned good at what we did, especially since doing our jobs meant bucking the prejudices of one of the oldest good-old-boys clubs known to man, the small-town police department.

I stirred sugar into my coffee and lifted the disposable cup to Darcy in mock salute. "Back to a life of drama and high adventure."

I was halfway to my office when Adler's voice crackled over the radio. "Contact Detective Skerritt. I've got a signal seven here. And I'm gonna need Animal Control on this one, too."

"Tell him to ring me on a landline," I called to Darcy. "No need to alert all the little old ladies glued to their police scanners that we have a dead body in Pelican Bay. Let 'em read it in tomorrow's *Times*."

When I arrived at the address on Grove Street, just a few blocks from the station, Adler stood out front beneath the streetlight, listening to an elderly woman with her hair in rollers, who wore a shapeless shift of floral polyester and rubber thong sandals in Day-Glo pink. She spoke like a Chatty Cathy doll wound too tight and pointed first to the address where we stood, then to the house next door. Adler scribbled furiously on his clipboard.

I scanned the quiet residential street, overhung with live oaks and camphor trees that puddled the street with darkness between the streetlights. A full moon, framed by tall palms, floated in the cloudless sky, and the sea breeze retained remnants of the day's heat. The night was a chamber of commerce dream, the kind tourists paid thousands of dollars to enjoy. If the signal seven turned out to be a murder, the chamber was not going to be happy. Pelican Bay's homicide rate was the lowest on Florida's West Coast.

The only sounds besides the high-pitched chatter of Adler's witness were the papery rattle of palm fronds in the breeze, raucous laughter from a too-loud television down the block, the blare of an approaching siren, and the piercing wail of an unhappy baby. Its cry made the hair stand up on the back of my neck.

The house where the body had been reported was unlighted. A car, too shrouded in darkness to identify, stood in the carport. Everything else appeared normal, until I realized the baby's cries emanated from the unlighted building.

I interrupted Chatty Cathy's monologue. "Is there a kid in there?"

Adler shook his head and nodded toward the old lady. "This is Mrs. Eagleton, the one who called us."

The woman straightened her shoulders and thrust out her scrawny chest, hiking her shift to expose knobby knees. "Captain of the Azalea Acres Neighborhood Crime Watch. I take my job seriously."

An ambulance turned the corner at a clip and headed toward us, lights flashing. It slowed to a stop behind Adler's cruiser and throttled its siren mid-wail.

"You said she was dead." Mrs. Eagleton glared at Adler accusingly.

"Officer Adler," I said, "assist the paramedics, will you?"

Looking as if he'd been released from hazardous duty, Adler scurried to lead the paramedics toward the rear of the house.

"Now, Mrs. Eagleton, how did you happen to discover the body?"

"As crime-watch captain, I keep my eye on the comings and goings of my neighbors. I saw Edith come home as usual—"

"Edith?"

"Edith Wainwright, the dead woman. She works for

the telephone company, and she came home at her usual time today. I didn't think any more about her until after dark, when I noticed she hadn't turned on her lights."

"Outside lights?"

Mrs. Eagleton shook her head, bouncing the pink foam rollers. "The light's always on in the living room, because Edith watches TV after supper or sometimes reads those self-help books. You know the kind."

I nodded. "Then what?"

"I went outside to check if her car was still there, and that's when I heard it." She jerked her thumb over her shoulder toward the house. "You can hear it yourself. Hard to miss, isn't it?"

The howling sawed on my tired nerves, and I longed for a switch to shut it off. "What is it?"

"Precious, Edith's Siamese. When I saw the car still there and heard Precious crying, I knocked on all the doors but Edith didn't answer. I tried going in, but the doors were all locked."

"That's when you called us?"

"Of course not." She shook her head until her rollers threatened to take flight. "I wouldn't waste your valuable time unless I was sure there was a problem."

Properly chastised, I plowed on. "Then what?"

"I went home for my flashlight, came back and looked in the windows to see if I could spot anything suspicious."

Azalea Acres, I thought, must be the safest neighborhood in the state. Nothing got by this one.

"As you can see," the woman said, "her draperies aren't closed."

Lamps had been turned on, and light streamed through the uncovered windows of the Wainwright house where Adler and the paramedics had gone inside.

Mrs. Eagleton pointed with a bony finger. "When I looked through the dining room window, there, I saw Edith on the floor in the hallway with Precious beside her. *That's* when I called the police."

The window she indicated was a wide, shallow opening at least six feet above the ground, and the woman couldn't hit five-two on tiptoe. "You looked in that window?"

"I used a stepladder. And my flashlight."

I felt a stab of compassion for Mrs. Eagleton's surviving neighbors. "Thank you. You've been very helpful."

"Is that it? This is a murder, isn't it? Aren't you going to ask me about suspects or motives or anything?"

"What makes you think it's murder?"

"Well, you're here, for starters." Her face took on a lean and hungry look.

"We're just following procedure. Probably a natural death. Most of them are."

Disappointment washed over Mrs. Eagleton's sharp features.

For starters, she'd said. "Any other reason you thought of murder?"

"No, it's just that—" She squirmed and curled her toes in her flip-flops.

"Just what?"

"Edith Wainwright was…well…"

Playing around on her boyfriend, wealthy with a greedy heir, drug dealer gone rogue? "What was Edith, Mrs. Eagleton?"

"Fat."

I shook my head, thinking I'd heard wrong. "Fat?"

She nodded, sending the pink foam into motion again.

"What does fat have to do with murder?"

"Fat people are repulsive. Lots of folks can't stand 'em. You know these crazy young hooligans these days. Don't need more than a dislike to kill somebody."

I clamped a lid on my disgust. "I'll be in touch, if we have any more questions." I turned my back on the woman and headed toward the house.

God save us all, I thought. Mrs. Eagleton's gaze

burned between my shoulder blades. If obesity was a motive for murder, over a quarter of the population was at risk of being whacked. I considered Mrs. Eagleton's skinny frame. Unless someone had a contract out on the terminally nosy, she, at least, was safe.

"What have we got?" I asked Adler as I entered the house.

"A strange case. No sign of forced entry, no sign of a struggle, no sign of anything except a dead woman and a damned screaming cat."

I plunged my hands into the pockets of my blazer and began my inspection. Edith Wainwright lay like a beached whale across the threshold between the living room and the hallway, her dark, sightless eyes staring at the ceiling. Neither the extra pounds nor the trauma of death disguised the beauty of the woman's face, the product of good bones, flawless skin and youth.

"God, she's just a kid," I said.

"Yes, ma'am. Twenty-two, according to the neighbor."

Younger than Adler. Less than half my age. Retirement was looking more attractive by the minute. "Can't you shut that cat up? And don't call me ma'am."

Luckily, I didn't know then that the Siamese would wail for almost two more hours before Animal Control showed up to carry it away.

Doris Cline, the medical examiner, arrived. Wearing gray sweats and Reeboks, with her thick gray hair cropped close and her trim body tanned and fit, she looked more like a physical education teacher than an M.E. as she started her preliminary examination.

"Poison. Cyanide," Doris said when she'd finished, and pointed to a thin trail of vomit at the corner of the victim's mouth. She stripped the latex gloves from her hands. "That musty, acrid smell confirms it. Time of death probably between 5:30 and 6:30 p.m."

"Any idea how the poison was administered?" I scanned the room for a syringe, a glass, plates or other utensils, but found nothing.

"Ingestion," Doris said, "judging from the condition of her mouth and pharynx."

"Murder?" Continuing my search, I threw the question over my shoulder while Doris gathered her equipment and prepared to leave.

She shrugged. "From the looks of things I'd bet suicide, but finding out for sure, that's your job, my friend. I am going home to bed."

"Autopsy?"

"I'll call you when it's set tomorrow."

After Doris left, I combed the house for clues to why and how Edith Wainwright had died. The obese young woman apparently lived with only her cat for company. No signs of any social life, nothing but a bookcase of tattered paperback romances and a well-thumbed *TV Guide*. No signs of other occupants or visitors. The situation supported probable suicide.

I turned to the two technicians with the sheriff's crime-scene unit I'd asked Adler to call in. "I want a sweep of the entire house, especially the living room. Fibers, prints, the works."

"Gonna get a lot of cat hair," the younger member of the team mumbled.

While the older technician snapped photos of the hall and living area, I inspected the kitchen. Except for the cat hair, Edith Wainwright had been a meticulous housekeeper. Not a speck of dust or spot of grime in sight.

Magnets on the gleaming refrigerator door displayed pithy comments: "A world without men—no crime and lots of fat, happy women." Another proclaimed, "I can stand any frustration as long as the cookies hold out," and a third, "God must have loved calories because he made so many of them."

A woman after my own heart.

Adler ambled into the kitchen with a small lavender book. "Found this in the bureau in her bedroom."

I pulled a handkerchief from my pocket and grasped

the diary between thumb and forefinger. Poor kid. She'd obviously been a very private person. Her death had destroyed not only her life but her privacy as well. By the time my investigation was complete, I'd know Edith Wainwright's every secret. Feeling like a voyeur, I placed the diary on the kitchen table and turned the pages.

The book documented Edith's despair over her weight problem and her desire for a boyfriend, one Jeff Hadley in particular. But the rest of the entries didn't fit with suicide. The latest were upbeat, almost joyful, a pound-by-pound account of her weight loss.

And if her death had been suicide, where had the cyanide come from? Adler and I searched the house, the car and carport, the utility shed and the dark yard, but located no sign of the poison or a container. What I did turn up shot the suicide theory full of holes.

The base of a blender sat on the kitchen counter, and I found the blender itself in the refrigerator, filled with a liquid that looked like weak Pepto-Bismol. On the counter beside the blender stood a tall glass, an empty envelope of diet drink powder and three bottles of vitamin supplements.

I reconstructed the victim's last minutes. Edith comes home from work, mixes herself a diet shake, pours it in the glass. But the glass was unused, absolutely clean. Had she tasted the supplement from the blender and died? Or taken the vitamins?

I bagged the blender and the items on the counter and handed them to the CSU techs. "I need these analyzed ASAP, in case product-tampering's involved."

Six hours after first arriving at Edith Wainwright's, I eased my way through the door of my town house, mindful of sleeping neighbors. With nerves as raw as ground meat and my brain wired from too much coffee and adrenaline, sleep wouldn't come easy.

I climbed the stairs to the second-floor bedroom, peeled off my navy blazer and tossed it onto the quilted bedspread. I removed my blue Smith & Wesson .357 from its holster, placed it on the bedside table and set the alarm for 6:00 a.m., just a few hours away.

After hanging my canvas shoulder holster on a hook inside the closet door, I tugged off my khaki skirt and plaid blouse and kicked off my loafers. I was stuck in a time warp. Almost thirty years out of college, and I still dressed like a preppy coed.

At least I was consistent. The oversize PBPD T-shirt I chose to sleep in wouldn't be out of place in any college dorm. After grabbing a blanket from the foot of my bed, I opened the sliding glass doors to the balcony, wrapped the blanket around me and settled on the cushions of the lounge chair.

When my father died, I'd used the money from my inheritance to buy a small condo on the waterfront. Its living room opened onto a small lawn with a seawall that held back the waters of St. Joseph Sound. I figured my investment had saved me thousands in psychiatry bills. When the stress of my job mounted, I'd sit on the seawall or the bedroom balcony and watch waves lap against the shore. The lulling, white noise of wind and water almost always scoured away the tensions and frustrations of work.

Tonight, I counted on the soothing surf and sea breeze to ease my racing mind so I could sleep, but I didn't hold out much hope. My brain revved with the latest statistics. A serious crime was committed in Florida every three minutes. What bugged me most were the criminals themselves. Maybe one out of four was driven to violence by extenuating circumstances—fear, rage, hunger, drunkenness, stupidity—and, as a result, suffered true remorse over his deed. The other three-quarters terrified me with their coldness. Psychopaths, or sociopaths, depending on whether you subscribed to the nature or nurture theory, none possessed the milk of human kindness. Never accepting responsibility for their crimes, they lacked the capacity for rehabilitation. A few years in lockup under Florida's revolving-door prison system would send them out onto the streets again, meaner, smarter, more deadly than before.

Had Edith Wainwright committed suicide or had she been murdered by a cold-blooded psychopath? Her diary revealed no one who might have snuffed her in the throes of hot-blooded passion. And if her death was a random murder, I had a sicko loose who apparently killed for the thrill of it.

My instincts told me I was dealing with murder, the first in more than five years in Pelican Bay. I took a dim view of some crazy out there killing the people I was sworn to protect and serve.

The daughter of a doctor, I could handle natural deaths. With so many elderly living alone in our town, the department was often called by neighbors or letter carriers to check on people who hadn't been seen or heard from, who didn't answer their doors or phones. The victims had usually succumbed to strokes or heart attacks.

But Edith Wainwright was different. Young and getting her life on track, she shouldn't have died. The more I'd studied the scene and evidence, the more convinced I'd become that Edith's death was murder. Just a few crucial details were missing, like motive, opportunity and suspects.

North along the shoreline from my balcony, the lights of the marina twinkled in the morning darkness. I tried to pick out Bill Malcolm's cabin cruiser from among the distant masts and flying bridges. I considered calling Bill to discuss the case. An incurable insomniac, he was probably still awake. Bill functioned better on two hours of sleep than most people did on eight.

Too wired to sleep, I tugged the blanket closer to ward off the October breeze blowing off the sound, and thought about Bill Malcolm.

CHAPTER 2

When I first met Bill Malcolm twenty-two years ago, he had been a twelve-year veteran of the Tampa Police Department. His thick brown hair, blue eyes sparkling with humor, and the spate of freckles across his nose gave him the angelic look of a choirboy.

A few years later, advancing age and the stress of the job had erased the boyish appearance and sharpened his face into a maturity no less beneficent. In any bad cop/good cop scenario, Bill was always the good guy. His kindly face belied the shrewd mind beneath it and made him an interrogator to whom people opened their hearts as to a priest in a confessional, all because of the deceptive innocence in his crooked smile and artless blue eyes.

I had viewed his kindly appearance with relief when first assigned as his partner. But when we hit the streets in the College Hill district for our first patrol, Bill set the record straight.

"Look, Margaret—"

Outside my immediate family, only Bill called me Margaret. When I'd entered the police academy, I'd adopted Maggie as a nickname, thinking it sounded tougher than Margaret, only to discover that everyone was called by last name—or worse. Skerritt sounded tough enough.

Bill, steamed at having been assigned a rookie and a woman as partner, referred to me as Margaret, spoken with a snooty British accent. On really bad days, I was Princess Margaret.

"Look, Margaret," Bill had said that first day, "I'm not here to lead you around and open doors for you. And you're not here to strike a blow for women's lib."

"I don't—"

"Is it true you were a debutante?"

"Yes, but—"

"Shit, I'm stuck with a society dame."

"Listen, Malcolm—"

"No, you listen. We've got a job to do, and to be honest, having you as a partner scares the crap out of me. If trouble goes down, I want a backup who can pull a two-hundred-pound palooka off me, not a well-bred lady who knows the right fork at a dinner party and looks like a puff of wind would blow her away."

For the first several months we rode together, Bill's

attitude remained cold. He was polite, unlike many others on the force, but distant, and I recognized that distance for what it was. Wariness. Bill Malcolm believed that having a woman for a partner was going to get him killed.

Seven months after I started with the Tampa PD, we answered a domestic-disturbance call at an apartment in a public-housing project. As we raced up the walkway toward the building, a woman inside screamed in short bursts of high-pitched, staccato cries. Just before we reached the door, the yelling stopped abruptly.

Bill banged on the door with his fist. "Open up! Police officers!"

A small boy with terror-filled eyes and a tear-stained face pulled open the door and mutely stepped aside. On the floor in the middle of squalor and shambles lay a young woman with her eyes closed and blood oozing from a cut on her forehead.

From that point, events moved in fast-forward. Bill rushed to the woman and knelt to check for a pulse.

I keyed my mike. "We need an ambulance." I verified the address for the dispatcher.

Then all hell broke loose. The boy emitted a chilling, pulsating scream. The woman opened her eyes and latched onto Bill's arms in terror. And a man the size of a small house burst through the kitchen doorway behind Bill.

"I'm gonna kill you, bitch, and the pigs, too." The blade of the machete he waved above his head caught the light from the bare bulb of the ceiling fixture.

I drew my gun. "Drop the knife!"

The man headed straight for Bill.

I fired and thought I'd missed him, because he neither reacted nor slowed. I fired twice more in succession.

The man stopped abruptly, looked down in disbelief at the bloodstains blossoming on his grimy undershirt, and collapsed on top of Bill, who still struggled to free himself from the woman's grasp.

The drug-crazed husband died. His wife sued the department, claiming police brutality because I had shot him three times in the chest.

"She coulda just fired a warning shot or hit him in the leg," the woman moaned before the television cameras. "Now my poor baby boy ain't got no daddy."

The bogus charges were eventually dropped, but other results of the shooting were more lasting. When Bill extricated himself from beneath the dead man's bulk, and we'd subdued and handcuffed the woman who'd recovered enough to assault Bill with her fists, he'd turned to me.

"Nice work, Skerritt."

He'd continued to call me by my last name, until our relationship took a different turn after his divorce. The shooting at the housing project had been the beginning of the end of Bill's marriage. His narrow escape had confirmed his wife Tricia's worst fears.

"I can't spend every day waiting to see if you'll end your shift in a body bag," she'd told him, and filed for divorce.

The divorce hit Bill hard, but even worse, Tricia moved to Seattle and took six-year-old Melanie with her. Bill had weekend visitation rights, but flying to Seattle was costly. And later, seeing Tricia with her new husband, an accountant with a nice safe desk job, didn't help Bill's broken heart, so his trips west soon ended. For the next few years, Melanie visited for two weeks in the summer, and I accompanied her and Bill to Disney World, Sea World, Busch Gardens, and every other attraction within driving distance. When Melanie reached her teens, she began to resent her visits that took her away from her friends. Bill told her she needn't come, if she'd rather not, and had been devastated when she didn't.

I'd met Bill twenty two years ago, and I think I loved him from the start But I'd kept my emotional distance

Bill was a terrific friend, and that's how I intended to keep things. Divorce statistics for police officers were through the roof, and I'd never been good at relationships, not even within my own family. Especially not within my own family.

As for Bill, his daughter Melanie was now twenty-eight and married. Bill had been retired two years from the department. His brown hair had turned white, and he'd added a few pounds to his lanky six-foot frame. He'd traded his regulation uniform for khaki Dockers, knit shirts and boat shoes, but he still had the same engaging smile and innocent blue eyes....

And one of the sharpest minds in law enforcement, a source I intended to tap for the Wainwright case. Tomorrow, as soon as I'd grabbed a few hours' sleep.

CHAPTER 3

When I awakened, the first glow of sunrise tinged the waters of the sound a golden pink. By seven, I was at my desk at the station, typing the initial report on Edith Wainwright's suspicious death. After placing the completed form on Chief Shelton's desk, I dialed Mick Rafferty's extension at the crime lab.

"I know it's Saturday," I said when he answered, "but I took a chance you might be in."

"A house full of visiting in-laws from Boston convinced me I should catch up on my backlog. Now, Maggie, me darlin', what can I do for you this fine morning?"

"Cut the blarney and get me an analysis of the blender contents, that diet powder and the vitamins your team brought in earlier. If product-tampering caused this death, I have a list of authorities to alert."

"Analysis complete, darlin'. Nothing poisonous in

any of it. Unpalatable, nutritious, low in calories. Boring, but not deadly."

I pictured the grinning Mick, young and cocky with red hair and wall-to-wall freckles. Dress him in green and he'd pass for a giant leprechaun. "What about prints?"

"None so far, except those of the deceased."

"Fibers?"

"We're still combing through cat hair, but nothing yet. If I hit on anything, I'll give you a call."

"Thanks, Mick...darlin'."

At least Mick's report laid the tampering theory to rest. It also made the death more puzzling. I opened Edith's address book and copied the short list of names, addresses and phone numbers. Sending Christmas cards had been no chore for this kid.

The first person on the list, Tonya Wilson, lived a few miles away in Clearwater. The drive took only ten minutes through sleepy residential streets. I parked in front of a small concrete-block house with a lawn that needed mowing, then threaded my way between the Big Wheels and toy trucks on the walkway and rang the bell.

The Miami windows were cranked open to the cool, dry October air, and the sound of cartoons blared from a television somewhere toward the back of the house.

I rang the bell twice before a slender young woman with stringy blond hair, clutching a short kimono closed at her throat and looking half asleep, opened the door.

"Tonya Wilson?"

"Look, if you're a Jehovah's Witness, you're wasting your time. We're all good Baptists here."

"Detective Skerritt with the Pelican Bay Police Department." I shoved my badge through the rapidly closing door. "I need to ask a few questions. It won't take long."

Tonya hesitated a moment, then pulled the door open. "If you have an extra minute, I'll put coffee on. I don't function in the morning without it. Maybe you'd like a cup?"

I followed her through a cluttered living room into the kitchen. She placed a filter in the coffeemaker basket and filled it with fresh grounds.

I pulled my notebook from my pocket. "Do you know Edith Wainwright?"

"Edie?" Tonya was pouring water into the coffeemaker reservoir. "Sure, we work together at the telephone company. She's not in some kind of trouble, is she?"

"Depends on how you define trouble." This was always the hard part. "She's dead."

Tonya turned, wide-eyed, and poured water across the kitchen counter. "Holy shit!"

Colorful language for a Baptist. I made a note of her obvious surprise. She grabbed a dish towel and mopped water from the counter. "When? How?"

"Last night. It's what we call a suspicious death. That's why I'm here. What can you tell me about Edith's frame of mind the past few days, particularly yesterday?"

Tonya finished filling the reservoir, flipped the switch, then removed two mugs from a cabinet above the stove and set them on the counter. "Edie was flying high yesterday."

"Drugs?"

She looked shocked. "No, nothing like that. Drugs aren't Edie's style. She's as straight as they come. A regular Goody Two-shoes."

Tonya spoke of Edith as if she were still alive, a common reaction to sudden, violent death. "What did you mean by flying high?"

She raked thin fingers through her hair and pushed it off her face. "She was pumped up. Happy. All day long she was humming and singing. If I hadn't known better, I'd have thought she had a big date or something."

She poured coffee into the mugs and offered cream and sugar. I added sugar, then sipped the steaming liquid, hoping for a jolt of caffeine. "Did she date someone special?"

"Someone special?" Tonya laughed. "Edie doesn't date at all. She's...you know."

"Overweight?"

"A real blimp. She has a heart of gold, a gorgeous face and a voice like pure sex, but she used to weigh close to three hundred pounds."

"Used to?"

"For the past few months, Edie's been on this diet. One of those liquid things like Oprah lost all that weight on once. And it's working, too. She's a real fanatic about it. Won't look at real food, won't even eat a measly jelly bean."

But she'd ingested poison, I thought, and it hadn't been in her diet drink. "What can you tell me about Edie's friends, her family?"

"Edie's folks are dead. She never mentions any friends. I think she's pretty much a loner." Tonya stirred more cream into her mug, then held it, childlike, cradled in both hands as she drank.

"Would you say she's been depressed, suffering from stress from the diet, maybe?"

She blew on her coffee while she thought. "No, Edie's always quiet, but she's been happier since she started this diet than in all the years I've known her."

So happy she killed herself? Not likely. "What about enemies?"

Tonya giggled. "Not unless you count Old Pruneface. That's Mrs. Austin, our supervisor. She rides us pretty hard. Nobody likes her."

"Did Edith ever mention a Jeff Hadley?"

"Sure. Hadley's one of our linemen, and easy on the eyes, too. Has the kind of hot looks that make women crazy. We both talk to him almost every day. Edie and I are dispatchers."

"But Edith never saw him outside of work?"

"Not that I know of. She flirts with him over the phone, not so much what she says as how she says it, the sexy-voice thing. But that's all there is to it."

"Where were you between five-thirty and six-thirty last night?"

Tonya's mouth gaped, and she sucked air. "You don't think I—"

"I'm just gathering information."

She set down her mug and shoved her hair off her face again. "I picked up the kids at day care right after work and drove straight home. Clark, that's my husband, was already here. We ordered pizza and spent the evening watching television."

I gulped the last of my coffee. "If you think of anything else that might be helpful, call me at this number."

I dug a card out of my pocket, handed it to Tonya and turned to leave.

A sleepy-eyed young man, wearing only bikini briefs that left nothing to the imagination, stood in the doorway. His eyes widened when he saw me.

"Holy shit!" He leaped backward into the hallway and out of sight.

Another Baptist. I let myself out the front door.

An hour later, I was wiping sweat from my forehead and fighting a gagging reflex. The air-conditioning at the county morgue had died the day before, and while the maintenance trucks had been parked out front when I arrived, the system was obviously not yet repaired.

Worse than the heat was the overwhelming stench of antiseptics and decaying flesh. Beside me, Adler, witnessing his first autopsy, swallowed repeatedly.

Noting Adler's bobbing Adam's apple, Doc Cline halted her description of Edith Wainwright's vital statistics, stepped away from the body on the stainless-steel table and retrieved a galvanized pail from a utility closet.

She shoved the bucket into Adler's hands. "Don't make a mess."

Tinged green beneath his tan, he nodded and hugged the pail close to his chest.

Doris returned to Edith's clothed corpse and with gentle fingers examined scalp, torso and extremities. After removing and tagging the victim's clothing, she studied the entire body again.

"No overt signs of trauma," she announced.

While Doris extracted and weighed internal organs, I puzzled over Edith's death. If the young woman had committed suicide, what had happened to the poison container? And if she'd been murdered, why had someone wanted her dead? Maybe Edith's lifestyle hadn't been the quiet, reclusive one Tonya and Mrs. Eagleton had described.

"Stomach is empty," Doris said, "except for small traces of what appears to be chocolate."

Doris's crisp, clear voice jerked my attention back to the autopsy, just as Adler splattered the contents of his own stomach into the pail.

"My partner, on the other hand," I said, "appears to have enjoyed a hearty breakfast."

"Happens to the best of them." Doris threw Adler a sympathetic look. "I've had bigger men pass out cold, and regularly, not only their first time."

Adler groaned. "Don't give me any ideas."

The medical examiner removed her gloves. "A toxicological analysis will confirm whether my suspicion of cyanide poisoning is correct."

"You get the easy job," I said. "If it is cyanide, *I* have to figure out how it got there."

I left the M.E.'s office and drove back to Pelican Bay. No one answered the door at Karen Englewood's house on Windward Lane, the second address on my list, so I headed back to the station and took the scenic route along Edgewater Drive.

Thirty-foot Washingtonian palms towered over the roadway. To the west, St. Joseph Sound sparkled like a crust of diamonds in the morning sun. In the flats exposed by low tide, egrets and herons stalked their breakfast, while in the deeper waters of the channel, the pelicans that gave the town its name dived like clumsy circus clowns for fish.

Walkers and joggers crowded a paved path that wound through parkland amid pines and palms on the water's edge. I envied those whose Saturday morning held nothing more challenging than a seaside stroll. I turned my twelve-year-old Volvo, another purchase from my father's legacy, onto the narrow main street of the business district.

Pelican Bay formed where Pelican Creek emptied into St. Joseph Sound. Early settlers appreciated the beauty of the site and established a community there in the late 1840s, after Florida became a state. A cotton gin and rough-planked dock, where steamers collected crops of sea island cotton, sweet potatoes and oranges to transport north to the railhead at Cedar Key, had once occupied the waterfront. Today, a large marina covered the basin, where sailboats clustered like a forest of defoliated trees. Bill Malcolm moored his boat in their midst.

Beside the marina, Sophia's, a resort hotel and four-star restaurant, built like a Venetian palazzo, stood where Main ended at the water's edge. Main Street, its early-1900s buildings restored and newer buildings constructed in the same turn-of-the-century style, drew antiques-seekers from all over the world.

I don't care much for antiques, but I can understand why people flocked to stroll the tree-shaded brick sidewalks, wander through the dozens of shops and stop for cold drinks and sandwiches at the picturesque sidewalk cafés. All very pretty and good for tourism, but if I wanted a new pair of pantyhose or a light bulb, I had to drive to Clearwater.

I slowed to a stop where the Pinellas Trail intersected Main and waited while an athletic couple in black spandex skated by on their Rollerblades. The trail, a former railroad track converted to parkland and bicycle paths, stretched from Tarpon Springs south to St. Petersburg. By midmorning, it was already clogged with joggers and cyclists. A conduit for crime, Darcy called it, because roving gangs of teenagers on bikes sometimes robbed trail-users or adjacent homes and made fast getaways on the trail, particularly at night along the unlighted path.

When I entered the station parking lot, Chief Shelton's car stood in its reserved parking space. He never came in on Saturdays unless there was trouble. But murder was trouble enough to rouse him out of bed on a weekend.

When I reached my office without encountering the chief, I breathed a sigh of relief, but my reprieve was short-lived.

"Skerritt! Get in here!"

That the chief chose shouting down the hallway instead of using the intercom was a clear sign of his displeasure. I plodded into his office, followed by the curious stare of Kyle Dayton, the day-shift dispatcher.

"Shut the door!" Dressed in an electric turquoise shirt and plaid pants, the chief paced back and forth before the picture window that overlooked the downtown park.

I could never understand why some men chose to spend their leisure time dressed in ugly clothes and hitting a tiny ball with a stick. But I was certain at least part of the chief's rage came from the fact that his regular Saturday morning golf game had been delayed, if not canceled, by events of the previous night.

I started to speak, thought better of it and studied the plaques on the paneled walls: certificates of appreciation from the chamber of commerce, membership in the Rotary Club and a Paul Harris Fellowship. I'd seen them all before, but repeat scrutiny kept me from confronting the tall, angry man pacing his office like a caged jungle cat. He'd turn on me soon enough without my making the first move.

George Shelton had never forgiven me for suing the department for discrimination when they'd passed over me in the hiring process sixteen years ago. He'd liked it even less a year later when I won my case, and he was forced by the court to hire me.

Raised in the Georgia foothills, rumored to have belonged to the Klan in his youth, wounded and decorated in Vietnam, Shelton made it plain to all in his department that he regarded working in law enforcement a privilege accessible only to those macho enough to meet his entrance requirements, the major one being certain physical equipment that I lacked, although balls have been ascribed to me by a few fellow officers speaking figuratively.

Through my job performance and failure to cave in under both subtle and overt harassment, I'd gained a small measure of grudging respect from the chief over the years, but a crisis brought all his old prejudices boiling to the top. When Shelton felt pressure, he wanted a *man* he could count on to get his ass out of the sling.

He stopped abruptly and leaned forward with both hands spread upon the high-gloss surface of his desk. I tried to remember what my own desktop looked like underneath all my files.

"I've had a dozen calls already this morning about the murder last night." His voice was heavy with accusation. "The mayor, two members of city council and several residents of Azalea Acres. They all want to know what we're doing to catch this killer."

Rumors traveled faster than the speed of light in a small community like Pelican Bay. The presence of emergency vehicles and a CSU van on Grove Street had started tongues wagging, and the pressure was on the chief to nab the killer.

He glared at me, pale blue eyes burning under bushy gray brows. Sunlight from the picture window reflected off his bald head, producing a bizarre halo effect. The devil disguised as a saint.

"We haven't determined that it *is* murder." I kept my response low-key, as if speaking to an animal I didn't want to spook. "It could be suicide. I'm checking it out."

Or I would have been checking it out if I hadn't been standing there being reamed out like an incorrigible schoolgirl.

"You made detective over my better judgment, Skerritt. Don't screw this up and prove me right."

"I appreciate the vote of confidence, Chief." My voice rang with sincerity.

Shelton glared at me again, as if hoping for a wrong step so he could nail me for insubordination.

"I've been working alone since Carter moved to Memphis," I said. "I could wind this up faster if I had some help."

"I've pulled Adler off patrol to assist. I want both of you working around the clock on this. Understood?"

"Yes, sir." He'd done me a favor. Adler had the most potential of any street cop on the force. He'd be a help, not a hindrance, unlike others Shelton might have chosen.

"What are you doing about these home invasions?"

His snarling question renewed my irritation. I was on the wrong end of a kitchen-sink dressing-down. He was pissed and throwing everything he could at me.

"In a perfect world," I said with a sigh of genuine longing and a straight face, "all home invasions would be committed by Asian gangs, breaking into homes to complete teenagers' math homework."

Shelton, who never got my brand of humor, simply blinked.

"Anything else, Chief?" I added a saccharine dose of awed respect to my tone. He could push me all he wanted, but my infamous temper was well leashed. "I have an investigation to conduct."

"Keep me informed. I want a full report of your progress on my desk Monday morning. Better yet, I'd like a suspect behind bars by then." He dismissed me with a wave of his hand.

I resisted the impulse to salute. Shelton knew how to push my buttons, but I'd learned to choose my battles. I consoled myself with the knowledge that he'd attained his exalted position through the Peter Principle. A better politician than cop, he'd finally reached his highest level of incompetence. Shelton had never worked the streets. He couldn't solve a case if someone shoved the evidence under his chin and rubbed his nose in it.

I concentrated on breathing deeply to purge the hostility from my system. The chief's door slammed as I entered my office. He was probably on his way to the country club where he would assure his cronies that he'd read the riot act to his department. Then he'd play a leisurely round of golf while I logged the overtime.

Adler was waiting in my office. "What's next?"

I jotted down the name of Wainwright's doctor. "Check this guy out. See what he can tell you about the victim. Check his alibi for yesterday. And locate a phone company repairman, Jeff Hadley. Find out what he knows about Edith Wainwright."

I pocketed the keys to the Wainwright house Adler had handed me. "I'm going to search the crime scene again, in case we missed something in the dark last night."

"Locard's Principle?"

I appraised my assistant with respect. "The perp brings something to the crime scene and takes something away, according to Locard. We haven't found what the killer, if there was a killer, left for us. Not yet."

Adler, dressed in plainclothes, shrugged into a leather bomber jacket. "I'll check back here and let you know what I've turned up."

Lace curtains moved over Mrs. Eagleton's front window when I parked on Grove Street beside the flapping yellow crime-scene tape in front of Edith's house. Before I could climb out of my car, the neighbor emerged from her front door. She wore Bermuda shorts and a sleeveless blouse that exposed her scrawny legs and arms, tanned and weathered by age and sun. Her thong sandals slapped the pavement as she approached.

She had removed her pink rollers, but her hair retained their shapes, lying atop her head like gray sausages that wiggled when she walked.

I met her and continued walking toward her house, away from the crime scene.

She turned and fell into step beside me. "Have you caught the killer yet?"

"As I said last night, we don't know that there was a killer."

"You don't think it's suicide?"

"We haven't ruled anything out yet."

"It wasn't suicide." She sounded certain.

"Why not?"

"The kid was too damned happy. When she left for work the other day, I was watering my azaleas in the front yard. She waved and smiled and called 'good morning.' Never saw a fat girl so cheerful. Why would someone so happy kill herself?"

I kept walking until I reached the Eagleton front porch, then stopped and looked back toward Edith's house. The side and back of her home could be seen clearly from this vantage point, but Edith's front door was blocked by an enormous arborvitae growing beside the front porch.

I turned to Mrs. Eagleton. "Have you thought of anything that might help the investigation?"

"No, but I've alerted the neighbors, so if anyone saw anything suspicious, they know to report it." Her smug grimace might have been a smile, but the ragged tracing of lipstick that rimmed her thin mouth made her expression hard to read.

"I couldn't rouse any of the neighbors last night," I said. "Who lives on the other side of the Wainwright house?"

"The Kolinskis, but they're still in Chicago. They don't come south until after Thanksgiving. And across the street are the Myerses, but they're cruising the Bahamas until next weekend. I'm watching their house while they're gone." She reached into her blouse pocket, took out a pack of Camels and offered me one.

I shook my head and studied Edith's front door. With the other neighbors away, someone could have come and gone there and not be seen, even in broad daylight. "You've been a great help, Mrs. Eagleton."

I left her basking in the sunlight on her front steps and puffing a cigarette. The woman had to be at least eighty. So much for the health hazards of smoking and too much sun.

I ducked under the yellow tape and strode up the walk to the front door. It was flanked by jalousie windows on the right, and beneath them sat two folding aluminum chairs with frayed nylon webbing. A massive clay pot filled with ferns stood between the chairs and the door. As I approached the porch, something gold glistened among the ferns.

Using a pencil, I snagged a piece of thin gold twine and lifted it out of the planter. The twine, its ends tied in a bow, was threaded through a plain white tag the size of a business card.

"Congratulations, Edith, from Karen Englewood" was typed on the card. The capital E had a large nick in the bottom serif.

"Did you find something?" Mrs. Eagleton strained against the tape along the front of the lot, trying to see what I held.

"Just a piece of trash."

I dropped the twine and the card into a handkerchief and slipped them into my pocket. I'd check the rest of the house and yard before I left, but I had a feeling that I'd already found what I was looking for.

CHAPTER 4

The October sun beat on the brick walks when I stopped at Scallops, a sidewalk café on Main Street. After leaving the Wainwright house, I'd interviewed the elderly victims of last night's home invasion, but they'd been unable to provide any more information than they'd already given Adler.

A pert young waitress in short-shorts and a too-small T-shirt, with the café's seashell logo emblazoned across her ample breasts, took my order.

Saturday antiques-hunters crowded the street, but I paid little attention to the sunburned throngs. I sipped iced tea with lime juice, ate the house specialty of turkey breast *en croissant* with sliced cucumber and alfalfa sprouts, and contemplated the card I'd found on Edith Wainwright's porch and its possible relevance to her death.

Forming conclusions early in an investigation leads to pitfalls, so I concentrated only on the facts. The pristine condition of the card indicated it had been dropped recently, and the twine, in addition to the card's congratulatory message, indicated it might have been attached to a gift of some sort. A small gift, judging by the length of the gold string.

Chocolates laced with cyanide?

I refused the waitress's offer to bring dessert, although the sight of a slim young woman at the next table, plowing through a concoction of fudge brownie topped with chocolate ice cream, hot fudge sauce, whipped cream and chocolate sprinkles almost broke my resolve.

The closer I came to fifty, the harder I had to fight to keep my weight within departmental guidelines. I didn't dare exceed them. Shelton would get a primeval pleasure from kicking my fat fanny off the force, as an example to others.

The drive to Karen Englewood's, just a few short blocks from my condo, took only minutes. Windward Lane intersected Edgewater Drive, and from the street in front of the Englewood house, I spotted the multicolored sails of windsurfers on the sound. The roar of Jet Skis barreling down the channel floated toward me on the breeze.

The day was pleasantly warm with just a hint of cooling in the wind, and the cloudless October sky shimmered a brilliant blue. Residents consider October the perfect time of year in Florida, but tourists seem unaware of the month's charm. Motels that proclaim No Vacancies for eleven months often stand empty in October. That suited me fine. Too many tourists already, and half of them returned home only to turn around and move to Florida permanently.

Some natives had resorted to bumper stickers, like the one I'd seen last week that read, "Welcome to Florida. Now go home."

All but a few dozen acres of the unending orange groves of my youth had been sold, subdivided and developed. What I remembered from childhood as sleepy country roads were now six-lane highways gridlocked with traffic. Deserted beaches where I'd played as a child were overshadowed by high-rises and thronged with people.

God, I felt old and wondered if every generation watched their world change and disappear before their eyes.

A woman close to my age answered the door at the Englewood address, a two-story Dutch Colonial built, like many of the homes near the waterfront, in the 1930s. Its pink stuccoed walls matched the flowers of the dwarf oleanders that lined the walkway.

"Karen Englewood?" I flashed my badge and identification.

"Oh, my God. It's not Larry, is it?" The woman's face paled, and she gripped the edge of the door as if to keep from falling.

"Take it easy, Ms. Englewood. I'm here to ask a few questions. Nothing to do with anyone named Larry."

Color returned to her face in a rush. "Forgive me. Larry is my son, and I was afraid something had happened to him. Please, come in." The woman struggled to regain her composure and stepped aside for me to enter. "We can talk in the Florida room."

I followed her through a dark entry hall and living room with drawn shades to a bright, glassed-in porch filled with white wicker furniture upholstered in a tropical print. Glazed pots of weeping figs and tree ferns turned the room into an indoor garden. The walls of jalousie windows, cranked open to the breeze, gave a sweeping view of the water at the street's end.

"You've lived in Florida awhile," I said.

"All my life. How did you know?" Karen waved me toward a wicker rocker at the end of a small sofa.

"You called this a Florida room. Northerners would call it a sunroom or sunporch."

"Very observant, but then I suppose that's your job." She sat on the sofa, reached into a basket on the floor beside it, picked up an embroidery hoop and began stitching with a large needle and red thread. "I hope you don't mind if I sew as we talk. I'm making Christmas presents, and Christmas will be here before you know it."

Karen Englewood was making a valiant if clumsy attempt to appear nonchalant, but she was obviously rattled about something. Two round spots of high color stained her cheekbones, and her hands trembled slightly as she stitched what looked like a Christmas stocking.

She was an attractive woman, one of those enviable people with good bones who manage to look more elegant as they grow older. A streak of gray cut a wide swath through her dark, lustrous hair, adding more drama than age to her appearance. She was dressed casually in a print dress with a fashionably short divided skirt. Like those of a true Floridian, her tanned legs were bare, and her espadrilles of colored straw matched her dress.

I felt suddenly gauche and clunky in my challis print dress, black blazer and loafers, then smiled inwardly at the turn my thoughts had taken. Twenty-two years of police work hadn't blinded my eye to fashion.

"I'm sorry to bother you on the weekend, Ms. Englewood, but I need some information on Edith Wainwright."

"Please, call me Karen." She smiled and dropped her needlework to her lap. Her nervousness had disappeared as if with the turn of a switch at the mention of Edith's name. "What do you need to know?"

"What's your relationship to Edith?"

"She's one of my clients."

"You're a lawyer?"

Karen laughed with an easy, pleasant sound. "I'm a counselor at the Pelican Bay Weight Management Clinic. Edith is enrolled in one of our weight-loss programs."

"What does your program involve?"

"We're connected with Pelican Bay Hospital, and Dr. Tillett—"

"Tillett?" That was the name of the doctor I'd sent Adler to track.

"Richard Tillett. He's our physician in charge. All our clients are medically supervised. Most of them have serious health problems, but Edith isn't one of them. She's young and healthy, anxious to complete her weight loss for cosmetic reasons, although she knows the positive effects of proper weight on her future health."

"I'm afraid Edith's future health won't be an issue. She died last night."

The color drained from Karen's face again. "My God, how? It wasn't connected to her fasting regime, was it?"

"We don't have the complete autopsy report yet. For now, her death is considered suspicious."

"Suspicious? As in foul play? That's ridiculous. Edith is one of the sweetest young women I've ever met. Who'd want to harm her?" Karen picked up the embroidery hoop and jabbed her needle into the fabric.

"That's what I'm trying to find out. Can you think of any reason why Edith might have wanted to harm herself?"

"Suicide?" Karen's deep blue eyes widened, then filled with tears that spilled onto her pale cheeks.

"We have to check out every possibility."

"If you'd asked me that question when Edith first came to our clinic five months ago, I'd have agreed that she had every reason to want to kill herself. She was so morbidly obese that simple everyday tasks, like bathing and dressing and getting in and out of a car, were a strain for her."

"What do you know about her relationships?"

"She had no close family. She was the only child of parents who died when she was a youngster. Her grandparents raised her, but they died recently."

"You don't believe she killed herself?"

Karen shrugged. "Edith suffered the ostracism and public torment that most obese people in our society face. Prejudice against fat people is apparently the last socially acceptable bigotry in our society." Her voice took on an evangelical fervor. "Edith was twenty-two years old. She should have been dating and going out with other young people, but she spent her life hiding, avoiding people, losing herself and her troubles in the fantasies of novels and television dramas."

"Sounds like a grim life."

"But lately she had hope. People with hope don't commit suicide."

I nodded. Karen's description of Edith matched what Mrs. Eagleton and Tonya Wilson had told me. "She was still obese, still withdrawn. Why are you so sure she didn't kill herself last night?"

"She had lost fifty pounds so far on her diet. She was feeling good, very optimistic about reaching her goal. Besides, as psychologist for the group, I encourage them to call me, any hour day or night, if they have problems. Edith didn't call, and she would have if she'd felt despondent." She wiped away a tear with the back of her hand.

"Did Edith socialize with others in the group?" I

struggled to remain objective. I liked Karen Englewood, but it was too soon to rule out suspects.

"No, but she was well liked by everyone. She was the youngest, you see."

"I'd like to talk with the others. Can you tell me their names and addresses?" I pulled out my notebook.

"Don't bother with that." Karen stood and crossed the room. "Give me a minute to warm up my copier and I'll duplicate my list."

She returned a few minutes later and handed me a copy of a typed sheet of names and addresses.

"That's all?" I said. "Just seven?"

"We keep the groups small so we can give our clients the individual attention they need." The wicker creaked as Karen settled back on the sofa.

"Just a couple more questions," I said. "Do you ever give congratulatory gifts to your clients? When they've reached a certain point in their weight loss, for example?"

A shadow of disgust crossed Karen's face. "You mean Skinnerian conditioning? Absolutely not. That's half the problem with our education system today. Makes people forget there's reward enough in doing something well. They want to be *paid* for it, too. Besides, my clients are so happy to be rid of those excess pounds, any token from me would be superfluous." She skewered her Christmas stocking again.

I flinched in sympathy for the sock and wondered if it was her surrogate for B. F. Skinner.

"One more question, then I'll be out of your way. Where were you between five and seven o'clock last night?"

At home, I punched the playback on my answering machine, and a deep male voice spoke. "Margaret, give me a call when you get in. I have a proposition for you."

I dialed Bill Malcolm's number and pictured him stretched out on the sofa in the lounge of his cabin cruiser, watching the University of Florida Gators football game on his tiny television.

"Margaret," he answered. "I'm glad you're home in time. How about a sunset cruise to Clearwater Beach and supper at Frenchy's?"

"You must be psychic. I need to talk to you. What time?"

"As soon as you can make it. You sound tired. You okay?"

"Nothing catching a killer won't solve. I'll fill you in when I get there."

I changed into white slacks, a navy pullover and

white canvas deck shoes and remembered Karen Englewood's elegant appearance. And her stumbling efforts to explain her whereabouts at the time Edith Wainwright died.

Karen claimed she'd had a quiet supper alone at home and had worked on her embroidery while she watched the television news, but she was a poor liar. Her hands had trembled, and she hadn't looked me in the eyes, not even when she said goodbye. Lying didn't automatically make her a killer, but it did place her on the list of suspects.

List? Who was I kidding? Karen Englewood at this point was my only suspect, and not a very good one. I had compared the typed list of clinic clients to the card I'd found on Edith's porch, but the type fonts didn't match. I hadn't expected them to. Most people sign their names to gift cards. The fact that Karen's had been typed indicated someone else had used her name. Unless Karen had typed it, hoping that's what others would believe.

Almost twenty-four hours had passed since Edith's death. My window of opportunity for nabbing a killer was narrowing. From everything I'd learned from Mrs. Eagleton, Tonya Wilson and Karen Englewood, I would bet my pension I was looking at murder. But I still had no idea who had killed Edith. Or why.

CHAPTER 5

Bill was waiting to cast off when I arrived at the marina. Saturday boaters, including parents with tired, crying children, sunburned and sand-crusted, crowded the dock. Several crews of deep-sea charter boats unloaded coolers, hosed down decks and secured lines.

I worked my way through the crowd to Bill's thirty-eight-foot cabin cruiser in the slip at the westernmost end of the dock. *Ten-Ninety-Eight*, police-radio code for "assignment completed," painted in bright red flowing cursive on the boat's stern, brought the usual smile to my face.

High tide made boarding easy, and I scaled the ladder to the flying bridge and sank into a swivel chair bolted to the deck next to Bill at the controls. He grinned but didn't attempt to speak over the thrust of the powerful engines. He slowly backed the boat from its slip into the channel that led to the sound, guided it into the Intracoastal Waterway and headed south toward Clearwater Beach.

On the western horizon, the sun slipped behind the tree line of Caladesi Island. The cloudless sky was deepening from a pale, watery blue-green to dusty rose. By the time we docked at the bayside motel owned by a friend of Bill's, the sky glowed tangerine.

"Volcanic dust," Bill said. "Makes for great sunsets."

He secured the lines and we walked two short blocks to Frenchy's, a rustic open-air restaurant with wooden picnic tables and the best grouper sandwiches on the beach.

While we ate fish and coleslaw and chugged a pitcher of draft beer, I gave Bill the facts of Edith Wainwright's death, careful not to color the narration with my own reactions.

"What do you think?" I said when I'd finished. I wiped tartar sauce from the corner of my mouth with a paper napkin.

Bill ordered key lime pie and coffee and waited until the waitress had cleared our plates before he answered. "No sign of where the poison came from, no suicide note, upbeat attitude of the deceased, assuming she wasn't manic-depressive. Sounds like homicide, but it's not conclusive. You don't have enough data yet."

"I still have six members of her diet group to interview. Adler's tracking down her doctor and a co-worker she had the hots for. Maybe they'll tell us something that will nail it down."

"Autopsy done?"

"Cyanide by ingestion. No other signs of trauma or illness. Sheesh, I hate murder. I'm getting too old for this."

Bill reached over and took my hand. "Give it up, Margaret. Your pension's vested, your condo's paid for. Retire, like I did."

I squeezed his hand, then released it and picked up my coffee cup. "And do what? I'd go crazy in a week."

"You could move in with me. We'll take another trip to the Bahamas, like last year. Hell, we could tour the whole Caribbean."

His voice was teasing, and I couldn't tell if there was an undercurrent of sincerity in his offer. His proposals of cohabitation and marriage had been a running joke in our relationship. But Bill had also lived a bachelor's existence for more than twenty years, the last two on his boat, and he seemed perfectly content with his single state. A part of me longed for him to be serious about marriage, but an equal part feared any change in our relationship might jeopardize our friendship and the comfortable limbo we both enjoyed.

"You know I could never live on a boat," I answered truthfully. "I don't love being on the water like you do. I'd rather view it from a distance from the balcony of my condo."

We'd had this conversation before, and this time wouldn't be the last. It had become a ritual, a never-ending pseudo-mating dance between two people who'd been burned too badly to risk commitment again, but who couldn't abandon hope completely.

"There's another option," Bill said.

I arched my eyebrows in question.

"You could put that degree in library science to use. The Pelican Bay Library would hire you. With your police experience, think of all the overdue books you could track down."

"I might just try that," I lied, then laughed at the startled look on his face.

The station, a low, modern building nestled beneath live oaks on the edge of a downtown park, looked more like a library or doctor's clinic with its tropical landscaping and tiled entryways. The second shift was leaving as I pulled my car beneath the soft sodium lights of the parking lot.

Chief Shelton's slot was empty. He and his wife,

Myra, a bleached-blond bimbo with an IQ in the double digits, attended the country club dance every Saturday night.

Adler met me in my office. "Finally got hold of Tillett's wife. The doctor's at a medical conference in Boca Raton. Won't be back until tomorrow afternoon."

"And Hadley?"

He consulted his notes. "He didn't know Edith Wainwright."

"That's odd. He worked with her, and Tonya Wilson said the two conversed by phone almost every day." I settled behind my desk and opened Edith's file.

"He said he only knew her by voice. Never met her."

I doodled on a notepad. "How did you read him?"

"I think he was telling the truth. When I told him she was dead, he didn't react much. But when I described her, his mouth fell open. He admitted he'd seen her before, 'waddling through the parking lot' was how he put it, but he hadn't known who she was."

"Alibi?"

He tossed a business card from the Blue Jay Sports Bar onto my desk. "Bartender verified Hadley and three of his friends came in before five on Friday and stayed until after nine."

I sighed. The more I knew, the less I knew. "And the good doctor?"

"Flew to Boca Raton Friday morning. Checked into the Boca Raton Club and Resort before noon, according to the desk clerk. He remembered the doctor's room wasn't ready." Adler twisted his head from side to side, as if to ease the tension in his neck. "Anything else you want done tonight?"

"Get some rest." I scratched an itch on the tip of my nose with the pencil eraser. If I didn't hook a substantial lead soon, I'd have a full-fledged case of hives. "But first thing in the morning, find out what you can about the doctor's whereabouts after he checked in. He could easily drive here from Boca in four hours."

"You think he's a suspect? What's his motive?" Adler scribbled in his notebook, then tucked it in the back pocket of his fitted jeans.

"Sexual harassment, malpractice, blackmail. The possibilities are endless. And until we rule someone out, everybody's a suspect."

After Adler left, I refueled on coffee and started making notes. I quickly polished off the list of known facts and began a list of what I needed to know. Just writing down the questions took a long time.

* * *

Sunday morning, the mockingbirds were singing among the blossoms of the golden rain tree beside my front door when I arrived home. I'd spent all night at the station, reviewing my notes until I'd fallen asleep at my desk.

Sunlight poured through the door into the foyer as I entered, illuminating the framed memorabilia hanging there. Most days I passed the grouping without seeing it, but today the tug of memory drew me to it.

A handsome young doctor with smiling eyes occupied the center frame. To the left was a picture of the same young man and a much younger me in a powder-blue evening dress, taken at our engagement party at the Pelican Bay Yacht Club. To the right hung a now-yellowed copy of a news article, recounting the tragic murder of Gregory James Singleford, my fiancé.

There were pictures of my parents and my sister, my diploma in library science from the University of South Florida, my certificate of graduation from the police academy, and a framed newspaper clipping of Bill and me in uniform, taken the day after I saved his life. The most recent photo captured me with Bill on the deck of the *Ten-Ninety-Eight*.

I reached up and touched Greg's photo. He'd been

killed shortly after that photo was taken. Working in the ER during his residency, he'd been mowed down by a crackhead with a Saturday-night special. I went through the denial stage of grief, refusing to believe he was dead until the day of his funeral. In the anger stage of grieving, I quit my job at the public library and enrolled in the police academy. I couldn't see spending my life safely and securely among books after the only man I'd ever loved had died so violently in a crime-filled world. Angry and idealistic, I had pursued my new goal with a vengeance. Only my fury over his senseless death had enabled me to survive the harassment, prejudice and the torture of physical training I'd encountered at the academy.

By the time I'd graduated, my anger had dissipated, replaced by a steady determination to prove my detractors wrong. I was going to be the best damned cop the Suncoast had ever seen—or die trying.

A decade later, the sudden death of my father from a stroke devastated me. I vowed then never again to set myself up for the heartbreak losing Greg and Daddy had caused. Burying myself in work was my prescription against emotional pain.

The ringing of the telephone intruded on my memories. I closed the front door, plunging my memory wall into darkness, and went into the kitchen to answer the phone.

The voice of Kyle Dayton, the day-shift dispatcher, greeted me. "You left too soon, Maggie. We got another dead one."

My stomach tightened. "When?"

"Call just came in from the paramedics. They say it looks suspicious."

"Do you have an ID?"

"Sophia Morelli, at her home at 1846 Santa Lucia Drive."

"Contact Adler and have him meet me there. I'm on my way."

I put down the phone. Morelli. Santa Lucia. I pulled from my jacket the list of names I'd copied from Edith's address book. Sophia Morelli was fourth on the list. Sophia Morelli on Santa Lucia Drive was also on the client list Karen Englewood had given me—a list with the names of seven people, two of whom were now dead.

CHAPTER 6

It was not a good day to die.

The nip in the salt-laden air of the season's first cold front stung my face through the open car window, and the sun shimmered in a cloudless sky. I contemplated never breathing such air or viewing such a sky again and suffered a sense of loss for Sophia Morelli, a woman I'd never met.

I turned off the highway and worked my way through a neighborhood of moderate, cinder-block homes with manicured lawns, inhabited mostly by retirees on fixed incomes, before reaching the impressive stuccoed pillars and ornate wrought-iron entrance to Pelican Point.

The heavy gates, usually closed, requiring residents to insert key cards for access, gaped wide. At the far end of the long, curving street, emergency lights of an ambulance and patrol car flashed in front of a house on the Gulf side.

Santa Lucia ran the length of Pelican Point, a wide spit of high-priced sand protruding into the Gulf of

Mexico on the north side of town. The locals called it Millionaires' Row because of its lavish, custom-built homes.

The intimidating mansions' flood-prone first stories of garages and storage rooms artfully concealed by architecture and profuse landscaping, rose twelve feet above sea level. Living quarters towered three and four stories above the street. I scanned the houses as I headed toward 1846. Money didn't guarantee taste. Styles ranged from art deco and gaudy Victorian to Key West and a bizarre mix of Byzantine and Gothic.

During the dog days of August, I'd paid a call to the Mediterranean-style mansion with arched cloisters and red-tiled roof. The rich might be different, but a few still beat their wives senseless when the urge hit them. The intimidated wives, who pressed charges only on Visa Platinum and American Express, refused to file complaints against their abusive husbands. Most were too scared. Others feared killing, or at least incarcerating, the goose that laid the golden eggs.

The Morelli house with lines and angles in the style of Frank Lloyd Wright was distinguished from others on the street by its wide Gulf-front yard. While the other structures crowded shoulder to shoulder on minimum setbacks, the Morelli mansion was centered on three lots that sold for half a million each. A tennis court filled the south yard, and terraced patios, bordered with hibiscus and ginger lilies, formed a buffer from the neighbors on the north.

Vehicles crowded the cul-de-sac at the peninsula's end, where paramedics loaded equipment as I parked. A few neighbors, gathered in a discreet group on the front lawn across the street, watched and murmured among themselves.

I met Joe Fenton coming out as I headed up the walk. The short, stocky paramedic yanked off his latex gloves and stroked a mustache that crouched on his upper lip like a dead caterpillar.

"Doc Cline's on the way," he said.

I jerked my head toward the house. "Anyone else home?"

"The husband. He's pretty shook up. Adler's with him."

I climbed the sloping walk to the second-floor entry. Wide double doors, inset with beveled glass etched with sea oats, stood open to a marble foyer. I followed the sound of voices, turned right and stepped down into a spacious living room with chalk-white Berber carpeting, ivory pickled woods and snowy upholstered furniture, whose cushions appeared never to have known a derriere. With its sliding glass walls stacked out of sight, the room opened onto the broad expanse of the Gulf of Mexico to the west and north.

At the room's far edge, a tall man slumped in a chair, elbows on his knees and his face buried in his hands. His dark hair and tanned arms and legs contrasted with his tennis whites and the room's furnishings. Adler's faded jeans and striped red-and-navy rugby shirt assured me I hadn't lost the ability to see colors.

The husband didn't look up when I entered. Adler pointed toward the foyer and moved to meet me there. "He's the only one in the house."

"What happened?"

"Lester Morelli said he was finishing an early breakfast. He has a doubles match with friends every Sunday at nine. Says his wife usually sleeps in until he's gone, but she was up early today."

"Where's the body?"

"The kitchen." Adler led the way through a door opposite the living room.

I followed, skirting a dining table large enough to accommodate twenty. We passed through a butler's pantry and entered a large kitchen overlooking the water. Appliances, ceramic-tile floors and European-style cabinets gleamed stark white.

The victim lay facedown, sprawled across the tile between the kitchen and the large bay window of the breakfast nook. Thick black hair obscured her face. She wore a short nightgown of sheer white cotton that had bunched around her thighs when she fell.

But she wasn't fat. Maybe fifteen pounds overweight, but not obese, as Edith had been.

"What do these people have against color?" The sterile white environment was getting on my nerves, already irritated by two suspicious deaths in three days.

I surveyed the room, taking in an overturned cup on the breakfast table and coffee staining the place mat and puddling on the bleached oak surface. On the counter beside the sink stood three plastic pill bottles, a blender, an unopened envelope of powdered diet drink and a glass, half full of what looked like water.

I turned to Adler. "Has the husband said anything else?"

"His wife came down to have breakfast with him. According to Morelli, she was all bubbly and smiling. Until she took her vitamins. Then she grabbed her throat, turned red in the face and collapsed."

I leaned down to examine the pill bottles without touching them. Multivitamin, magnesium and potassium supplements. I'd seen the same containers in

Edith's kitchen, but Mick had tested them and found only the contents listed on the labels.

"What then?" I said.

Adler consulted his notes. "Morelli dialed 911, but by the time the paramedics came, she was gone."

"Cause of death?"

"Her husband said she has a history of heart trouble. The paramedics called Doc Cline's beeper."

I shuddered. The all-white atmosphere of the house mimicked a Hollywood director's version of heaven, right down to the sheer milky drapery blowing in the morning breeze. Now Sophia had abandoned her stage set for the real thing. "Morelli tell you anything else?"

Adler shook his head. "The guy's shaking like a palm in a hurricane, and he's white as a sheet."

"At least he matches the decor."

I crossed to a doorway that opened out onto a balcony encircling the back of the house. A boardwalk connected the St. Augustine lawn to sand dunes anchored with sea oats and crossed to a broad beach of white-sugar sand. Unless the Morellis buttoned up the house at night and turned on a security system, anyone with a boat would have access to the property and the house.

"See that no one," I said, "disturbs anything until

Doris arrives. Then glean what you can from the neighbors. I'll see what else Morelli can tell us."

I went back into the living room to confront the grieving husband. The house bothered me. Its antiseptic living room looked like something from the pages of *House Beautiful*, without the tastefully arranged personal clutter usually featured in such layouts. A gigantic black-and-white photograph of sand dunes and cabbage palms, hanging above the white marble mantelpiece, was the focal point of the colorless room. Only a wedding picture, framed in silver on an end table, indicated real people had inhabited the place. A plump, dark-haired bride with attractive Mediterranean features and a radiant smile clutched the tuxedoed arm of a young groom with a handsome Latin face. Her form-fitting gown accentuated every curve, more than two hundred pounds' worth.

"I'm sorry for your loss, Mr. Morelli." I took a chair across from the man, who still sat with his face in his hands.

He lifted his head and stared at me, his bedroom eyes a deep caramel color with slightly drooping lids. He was more handsome than his wedding picture, with a strong, chiseled jaw and even white teeth; the only detraction from his looks were their perfection, as in too-good-to-be-true. And the pain in his eyes.

"And you are?" Irritation edged the sadness in his voice.

"Detective Skerritt."

"Detective? Do you always investigate heart attacks?" His hands shook until he clasped them firmly together. He studied his white knuckles for a moment, then moved his hands to the arms of the chair, where his fingers plucked at the loosely woven fabric.

"I'm sorry to bother you," I said, "but while we wait for the medical examiner to verify cause of death, I must ask some questions. They're just routine."

"I'll tell you what I can, but I'm not thinking too clearly right now." His glance traveled toward a door that connected the kitchen with the living room.

Heels tapping on marble sounded in the foyer, and I heard Adler direct Doris Cline toward the kitchen.

"Your wife's name?" I said.

"Sophia Gianakis Morelli." His voice cracked on a sob.

"Gianakis? George's daughter?"

George Gianakis's father had founded Sophia's restaurant and resort on the waterfront. And George had made millions in real estate and development before his death. Sophia had inherited it all. I thanked my mother's endless accounts of Pelican Bay's elite social scene for that bit of information.

Morelli nodded. "You wouldn't have a cigarette, would you? I gave them up a month ago, but now... Jesus." He combed his fingers through thick dark hair untouched by gray, then returned to tugging the threads of the chair arms.

"Sorry," I said. "I never picked up the habit. How old was your wife?"

"Thirty-nine." A ghost of a smile flickered across his ravaged features. "Really."

Either Morelli hit the Grecian Formula often or was much younger than Sophia. "And you?"

"Does it matter?"

"Just routine, for identification."

"Thirty-one."

"Any children?"

"No." He exhaled a deep, shuddering sigh. "When we were first married five years ago, Sophia's health was so poor, her doctor advised against pregnancy."

No children. Whoever Sophia's beneficiaries were, they stood to gain millions. "Because of her heart?"

"That, high blood pressure and diabetes, all complicated by her weight."

"So you were expecting something like this?"

"Hell, no." He sprang to his feet with the grace of an athlete and turned away, staring out over the water. "For the past two years, her health had improved. She lost a ton of weight and brought her diabetes and blood pressure under control. We were beginning to talk about having a family, adopting if the strain of pregnancy still proved too dangerous."

Emotion made his last words almost indistinguishable, and his shoulders shook.

My heart told me to leave the poor guy to his grief, but my head had work to do. My fatigue had returned. Too many victims, too much pain, and me with an orchestra seat to it all. Maybe Bill was right. I should take that library job. In books there were more happy endings.

"What happened this morning?" I said.

His muscles tensed. "I already told the other one."

I stifled my sympathy. "Tell it again."

He turned to face me and jammed his fists in the pockets of his tennis shorts. "I was finishing breakfast. I always play tennis early on Sunday mornings, and Sophia sleeps late. Today she surprised me by coming down early."

"Did she seem ill or mention feeling bad?"

He shook his head. "She said the day was too gorgeous to waste in bed. She kissed me good morning, then went to the sink and took her vitamins."

"The ones on the counter?"

"Yeah. As soon as she swallowed them, her face flushed and she grabbed her throat. She couldn't talk. I thought she'd choked, so I tried the Heimlich maneuver. She passed out, and I laid her down to call for help."

A tear ran down the sharp angle of his cheek, and he bit his lower lip in an obvious effort to regain control. All his good looks and money couldn't erase the fact that his wife lay dead on the kitchen floor.

"That's all for now," I said. "Is there someone I can call to stay with you?"

"Ted Trask, next door." His voice trembled. "We were supposed to play tennis this morning."

I left him and went to the kitchen, where I found Doris Cline, dressed for church in a red silk suit.

"You'd better call CSU," Doris said. "You've got another poisoning on your hands."

I welcomed the pale greens and blues of my condo after the colorless atmosphere of the Morelli house. Bill called my decor tourist-class-Florida-hotel, but the pastels, the natural rattan-and-wicker furniture and framed beachscapes provided a soothing counterpoint to my rough-and-dirty job.

I undressed and stood in the shower and let the pulsing water beat against my aching muscles while I tried to sort out the morning's events.

Doris Cline's announcement had come as no surprise.

"It wasn't her heart?" I'd asked.

"Her bum ticker could have been a factor, but I doubt it. The signs are the same as Wainwright's, and Edith's autopsy confirmed cyanide poisoning."

"Any other signs of trauma?"

"Nothing overt," Doris said. "I'll know more after the autopsy."

In the Morelli kitchen, seagulls screamed outside the windows. I felt like screaming myself. I knew the criminal mind, but I'd never understood it. How could anyone justify taking another's life? I resisted the urge to smash something. On my salary, I couldn't afford to replace anything in this upscale house.

"What do you know about Dr. Richard Tillett?" I asked Doris.

"He's well respected in the medical community. Why?"

"I have a list, a support group of seven patients at

his weight-loss clinic. Two on that list are now dead. Murdered."

Doris smoothed her jacket over trim hips and picked up her bag. "A serial killer?"

"Or product-tampering." The beginning of a headache blossomed behind my eyes. "Remember the Tylenol murders? Just because we didn't find poison in Wainwright's remaining vitamins doesn't mean it wasn't there to begin with. This one took vitamins just before she died."

Doris threw me a sympathetic smile. "Better contact the FDA so they can alert the manufacturers to issue recalls. I'll have a report for you by the end of the day."

"Thanks. Let's do lunch soon."

"Right." Doris laughed at our standing joke. We both considered ourselves lucky when we had time to catch a sandwich on the run.

After Doris left and the crime-scene unit arrived, Adler and I waited for a warrant before canvassing the house and grounds. I'd already notified Karen Englewood, who promised to call the five surviving members of her group to warn them not to take their vitamins. I arranged for a uniformed officer to collect the bottles to be checked for tainted capsules. Dr. Tillett's wife informed me when I called that her husband would be home after lunch. I made an appointment to meet him there at two o'clock.

Examination of the Morelli house provided little more than further confirmation of the couple's opulent lifestyle. And the fact that Lester and Sophia occupied separate bedrooms. The floor above the living area, reached by elevator, consisted of two spacious suites, where each adjoining bath was bigger than the entire second floor of my place.

An antique white Swedish sleigh bed heaped with lace-covered pillows centered Sophia's room. The only touch of color came from the splash of deep blue skies in the James Harrill prints of Greek-island villages that lined her walls. On her desk, next to a diary that documented her daily weight and calorie intake, lay a one-way airline ticket to Athens for the following Tuesday.

Lester's room was equally colorless, but in subtle shades of gray, accented with stainless-steel and smoked glass. Weights, a treadmill and rowing machine filled half of his gigantic bathroom.

I took the elevator to the fourth floor and inspected the two remaining rooms, Sophia's morning room with windows on three sides overlooking the bay and Gulf, and Lester's study. The order on his desk indicated Lester was either excessively neat or the desk was decorative rather than functional. A giant-screened television dominated the one windowless wall, and faint traces of cigarette smoke hung in the air.

I checked the desktop, looking for a companion for the airline ticket.

"What do you think you're doing?" Lester entered the room and strode toward me. Anger had replaced his grief.

"Did you and your wife get along?"

"What the hell kind of question is that? My wife is *dead*, and you're prying into my home and life? I think you'd better leave."

He moved closer, and I backed away, placing the wide expanse of the desk between us. "You've seen the search warrant, Mr. Morelli, and I have to determine who poisoned your wife."

"Poisoned? Sophia? By vitamins? You're crazy. She's been taking those for years. It had to be her heart. Her doctor will confirm it."

The guy was in major denial. "The medical examiner knows her stuff. Your wife died from cyanide poisoning."

He shook his head and started around the desk. "Are you going to leave, or do I have to call my attorney?"

"Do you need an attorney?"

"I have the right to grieve in peace, without this intrusion." His words blazed with anger, but the rigid line of his mouth softened and wavered, like a kid trying hard not to cry.

"Look," I said, "I don't want to make things any more difficult than they are. Can we just sit down and clear up a few things? Then I'll leave."

I eased around the desk, grasped his elbow and led him back into the morning room. Its three sides opened to a breeze that expanded the sheer snowy draperies like sails. Bleached oak gleamed beneath our feet, and the water view created the illusion of riding a ship at sea, a peaceful contrast to the violence two floors below.

Morelli collapsed into a corner of the white rattan sofa like a man whose bones had given way. "What do you need to know?"

"How would you describe your relationship with your wife?"

"I loved her." His voice broke, and he choked out his words. "I told you, we were planning a family."

I took a stab in the dark. "Then why was she leaving you?"

His head snapped up and his eyes clouded, confused. "Leaving?"

"I found a one-way ticket to Athens on her dressing table."

He relaxed against the sofa back. "She was going to visit her cousins."

"For how long?"

"It depended on the atmosphere when she got there. Greek families are very close, but they can also be…tempestuous." He pressed a fist against his lips. "Jesus, now they'll all be coming here. To her funeral."

"Did your wife have any enemies?"

He leaned toward me and clasped his hands between his knees. A sunbeam hit his cinematic good looks like a klieg light. "Everyone loved Sophia. She had the disposition of an angel."

Only the most embittered spoke ill of the dead. "She never quarreled with anyone?"

He laughed with a crude snort that clashed with his movie-star image. "Only her Uncle Vasily. They fought like cats and dogs."

"Over what?"

"When George Gianakis died ten years ago, he left Sophia everything—the hotel, the restaurant, the bundle he made off real estate." He glanced around the room, then out across the Gulf. "Not that any of it will do her much good now." He buried his face in his hands.

"Vasily?" I prompted.

"He was always pissed that George hadn't left him a bigger share of the family pie. After all, Vasily worked all his life in the business, but always in the shadow of his older brother, their father's favorite."

"Family feuds are one thing. Murder's another."

His dark eyebrows drew together in a frown. "What are you saying?"

Murder is an ugly business. Not just the act itself, but the motives and passions that it springs from. Most people don't like to face them, and Lester Morelli was no exception. "Can you give me Vasily's address? I want to question him."

A sardonic smile lifted a corner of his mouth. "If you can track down Vasily, you're a hell of a detective. He's been dead five years."

Solving a murder—unless it's one of those stupid acts of violence done in a moment of uncontrollable rage, like the man last summer in Tampa who stabbed his wife with a barbecue fork when she complained her steak was overcooked—is like wandering a labyrinth and running up against one dead end after another until you work your way through to an opening. I abandoned Vasily and chose another path. "Who stands to profit from your wife's death?"

"I can't accept the fact that Sophia's gone, much less that someone intentionally..." He shook his head and gazed across the water, apparently still dazed.

I waited. Lester Morelli was either devastated or an Oscar-class performer. He looked back at me as if surprised I was still there.

"You want to know her beneficiaries?"

I nodded.

"Until last week, I was her only beneficiary. In the event of Sophia's death, everything would have gone to me. The house and money and the restaurant and resort. She thought it only fair, since I've managed the business for the past five years."

"And now?"

"She changed her will. I agreed, of course. After all he'd done for her, how could I not? He saved her life."

"He?"

"Dr. Tillett. Sophia wanted to thank him."

"And the extent of her gratitude?"

"She bequeathed a million dollars to Richard Tillett and the Pelican Bay Weight Management Clinic."

CHAPTER 7

Later, at noon, I surveyed the interior of my refrigerator, withdrew the last container of fat-free blueberry yogurt and a Diet Coke, and added a couple of stale chocolate chip cookies for a three-course meal. For me, a complete dinner consisted of a frozen entrée zapped in the microwave and salad from a bag. Fortunately, no one else depended on my cooking to keep from starving to death or dying from culinary boredom.

In the tiny galley of his boat, Bill could whip up an eight-course feast, a skill that had me threatening to call his bluff on his marriage proposals on several occasions when I'd felt weak and hungry.

I sat at the dining room table to complete my notes on the Sophia Morelli homicide while I ate. Lester had made no attempt to hide his status as Sophia's heir. The fact that Tillett was also a beneficiary created a fork in the money trail. But the only connection either Lester or Tillett had with Edith Wainwright was through the clinic.

I carried the phone to the table and punched in Adler's number. The grogginess in his voice told me my call had awakened him. We'd both be catching whatever rest we could before this case was closed.

"Start tracking down everything you can on Wainwright's next of kin," I said, "and any other friends we might not know about."

Silence filled the other end of the line for a long moment. "I'll get on it first thing in the morning."

"Dammit, we've got two murders already and a possible serial killer. We can't afford the luxury of weekends off."

His hand must have covered the mouthpiece, because I could hear only a muffled exchange of words. I knew nothing about Adler's home life and wondered what I'd interrupted.

The line cleared. "Today's my little girl's first birthday. We're having a party this afternoon. Would you like to stop by?"

I remembered Bill and Tricia and Melanie and their shattered family. And Sophia Morelli and Edith Wainwright and the children they would never have. Maybe

Chief Shelton was right. I was too soft to be a cop. "One of us has to work, but I'll drop by if I can."

"I'll start digging into the info on Wainwright as soon as the party's over."

"One other thing—"

"Yeah?"

I heard the hesitation in his voice and sympathized with the guy, his wife and daughter tugging on one side, his job on the other. No wonder so many police marriages went bust. "Find out if Edith had a will."

I'd no sooner clicked off the phone than it rang again. "Skerritt here."

"That's an odd way to greet your mother." Her soft, cultured tone held its usual lick of disapproval.

"Sorry, Mother." I'd called her Mom once as a child, and she'd reprimanded me for sounding common. "Can't talk now. I'm on my way to interview a suspect."

"On a Sunday?"

My inner child, as the psycho-babblers called it, winced, but the outer me had a hide like a gator. "I'll place lack of social niceties on the top of my profile for the killer."

She sighed, as only Mother could. "I wanted to remind you about tomorrow night's dinner at the club.

Seven o'clock. Detective or not, you are still a member of this family."

My inner child squirmed again. Mother knew how to trowel on the guilt. I hated dinners at the yacht club even when I had the time. I got the bends every time I ascended from the depths of police work into the rarefied atmosphere of Pelican Bay's social elite.

"I'll come if I can, but we've had two homicides over the weekend, and I'm swamped."

A long, disapproving silence resonated in my ear.

"Maybe you can help me out," I said. "What do you know about Richard Tillett?"

"Margaret, you know I never gossip."

And the pope never prays. "You're always such a good judge of people," I schmoozed. "Just tell me what you think of him."

"He and Stephanie belong to our club. They're there regularly on family night. You'll see them for yourself tomorrow."

"If I can make it. Anything else on Tillett?"

"Well…"

Mother loved furnishing the latest skinny on Pelican Bay's upper crust, but only after believing it had been dragged from her by wild horses. "I need to know.

Two of his patients have already been killed. Others might be at risk."

"Oh, dear. How awful. Your father never lost a patient to murder—"

"Not now, Mother." If I let her start, she would reminisce about Dad's cardiology practice for hours. "About Dr. Tillett?"

I could picture her, sitting by her ruffled dressing table, cupping long, manicured fingers around the mouthpiece and bending her coiffed white curls closer to the phone.

"There have been rumors," she whispered. "Money problems. Seems the young doctor has taken up playing the greyhounds. Spends all his spare time at Derby Lanes."

"Thanks. I knew I could count on you."

"You're welcome. And can I count on you, Margaret? After all, in case you've forgotten, tomorrow is my birthday."

With that last zinger, calculated to inflict maximum guilt, she hung up on me.

The Tilletts lived in Orangewood, a complex of high-priced homes George Gianakis had developed on gently rolling land around a lake east of town in what had been the last of Pelican Bay's citrus groves.

The paved entry road, formerly a sandy track to a

rustic fruit stand, was marked by brick walls and black wrought-iron street lamps. A wide median, filled with crepe myrtles, azaleas and Indian hawthorn, divided the street. Although not as pricey as Pelican Point, the houses with soaring entries, palladium windows, landscaped lawns and triple-car garages didn't come cheap. Tillett's annual mortgage payments probably exceeded my yearly income.

I turned right at the first corner and pulled up against the curb beside the third house, a sprawling one-story with multiple gables, tall windows and a sun-bleached exterior needing paint.

Richard Tillett, a pleasant-looking man in his early forties with intense blue eyes, answered the door. He wore Bermuda shorts and a knit shirt that showed off his William Shatner build and deck shoes without socks. A small boy with golden curls and the face of a Botticelli cherub clung to his leg. Tillett picked up the child, and I followed them through a tiled foyer into a sunken living room.

A slim young woman with dark hair and eyes and a worried crease between her eyebrows hurried into the room. "Jeremy, come with me. You mustn't bother Daddy."

Tillett smiled, but the expression never reached his eyes. "My wife, Stephanie."

"We spoke on the phone," I said.

"Yes. I'll leave you to your business," she said in a snappish tone, took the child without looking at her husband and hurried from the room.

The tension in the air was so thick I could lean on it.

"Please forgive Stephanie. She's upset by this. We all are."

He indicated the sofa and sat opposite me on the U-shaped couch, crossing first one leg, then the other, before finally resting both feet on the floor and grasping his bare knees. "Any idea who killed my patients?"

"I'm hoping you can help me."

The man was a collection of jangled nerves, but his clear gaze met mine without wavering. His fingers flexed and tightened on his kneecaps. "Karen Englewood called. She met your officer at the clinic and turned over our supply of vitamin supplements and diet-drink powder for testing. She's also alerted all our patients."

"Who, besides you and Karen, had access to those materials?" I dragged out my ubiquitous notebook and clicked the nib on my pen.

Tillett shrugged. "Everybody. They weren't locked away. Any patient could have wandered unnoticed into the room where they were stored. If Gale was busy, she often sent them in to pick up their own supplies."

"Gale?"

"Gale Whatley, my office manager. Besides her and Karen, there's Naomi Calvin, my nurse, and Gina Peyton, the lab technician."

The clinic seemed to be the connecting factor in the two murders, and the list of people involved in the clinic continued to grow. "I need to meet with your staff and the group that Edith and Sophia belonged to."

"Tomorrow at five is our regular session. Is that soon enough?"

I nodded and scribbled a reminder in my notebook. "You were in Boca Raton all weekend?"

"At an endocrinology seminar." His response tumbled out too fast, like a man trying to cover for himself. "I delivered a paper on metabolism."

A chill current of air emanated from the cooling vents, but a thin sheen of perspiration coated Tillett's broad forehead. I was getting strange vibes from the good doctor. His fingers clenched his legs, creating depressed white ovals on his tanned skin.

"So someone from the seminar can verify your whereabouts from Friday noon until you caught your plane home this morning?"

"Not exactly." He cleared his throat with a nervous cough. "I checked into the resort early to work on my speech and didn't leave my room until the meeting started at ten yesterday morning."

"The seminar ended today?"

"No." He crossed his arms over his chest, tucked his hands beneath his armpits and stared out the glass doors that opened onto a swimming pool. "There was a banquet last night. It lasted late, so I flew out today. I can give you a list of attendees. They'll verify my presence."

Sweat trickled down one side of his face, and he hunched his shoulder to wipe his face with his sleeve.

"This group the victims were in," I said, "was there any bad blood among the members?"

His pale eyes met mine again. "Karen can tell you that. I see patients individually, so I don't know how they interact."

"Did anyone on your staff have a problem with either Edith or Sophia?"

He surged to his feet and paced the floor behind the sofa before leaning toward me with his hands on the sofa's back. "Edith and Sophia were two of the most gentle, nonthreatening women anyone could hope to meet. It's like they invented politeness. How anyone could—"

Something clicked. I saw it in his eyes. "What?"

He shook his head. "It's probably nothing."

"There's no way to know what might be helpful in a case like this."

"Brent Dorman, the lab technician who did blood and urine workups for the clinic."

"Did?"

"I fired him two weeks ago."

Bingo. A disgruntled employee. "Why'd you let him go?"

"He was rude to my patients. He told Edith she was so big, dogs probably followed her around for shade. She cried when she told me. When I confronted him, he displayed an almost pathological hatred of obese people, so I had to let him go."

"Did he make any threats? Cause any trouble?"

Tillett returned to his seat, the most relaxed he'd been since my arrival. "Dorman's a bodybuilder, the strong, silent type. He looked like he wanted to hit me, but he just glared, then took off. I haven't seen him since."

A network of minute creases framed his eyes, and deep furrows ran from his cheeks to the corners of his mouth. Now that his nervousness had passed, signs of fatigue erupted everywhere, from the slump of his shoulders to the redness in his eyes. Must have been a hell of a seminar.

"How old are you, Doctor?" When doctors looked younger than I did, I really felt my age.

"Forty-three. Why?"

"For my report. I don't need to tell you about paperwork, I'm sure."

"Hell, I'm buried in it. I spend more time with insurance forms than with patients."

"How long have you practiced in Pelican Bay?"

"Fourteen years. I opened my clinic ten years ago." He spread his arms along the back of the sofa.

"Are you aware of Sophia Morelli's provision for you and your clinic in her will?"

The bright flush of color that rose to his hairline gave me his answer before he did. "It's an occupational hazard."

"Bequests from patients?"

"Patients who become infatuated with their doctors." His flush deepened. "Sophia was very grateful for the help we'd given her, but she also seemed starved for affection and attention. She received plenty of both at the clinic. The bequest, she said, was her way of showing her gratitude."

"Didn't her husband give her affection and attention?"

"Lester Morelli is devoted to his wife. But the obese are pariahs in our thin-worshipping society. Often, if they're lucky enough to receive support from their families, that's their only positive reinforcement. They're all hungry, if you'll excuse the pun, to be accepted, to fit in."

Stephanie entered from a door behind her husband and laid a hand on his shoulder. He stiffened at her touch, then grabbed her hand and pulled her around beside him with a smile that seemed forced.

"Would you like some coffee, Detective Skerritt?" she asked. "Or iced tea?"

She didn't look at her husband, and I had the feeling I'd walked into the middle of a family feud with the combatants waiting for me to leave before resuming hostilities.

"Thanks, but I have work to do. Dr. Tillett, I'll see you tomorrow at five."

Stephanie walked me to the door. When it closed behind me, I paused, waiting for sounds of an explosion, but heard nothing. Maybe Stephanie Tillett was the type who expressed displeasure with icy silence rather than heated debate.

Sunday browsers crammed the Barnes & Noble at Sunset Point Shopping Center. In the children's section, I located a copy of *Pat the Bunny* for Adler's kid, but finding an appropriate gift for Mother wasn't as easy. Interviewing Tillett's staff and patients the next evening would make me late for her birthday dinner, but I couldn't arrive empty-handed.

After finishing my shopping, I called the station for Adler's address and drove to his southside neighborhood. Vehicles lined the curb in front of his place, a small house with gray siding and black shutters.

The Tillett and Morelli residences had seemed cold and uninviting, but Adler's had *home* written all over it. A wide porch stretched across the front like open arms. Rocking chairs, a wooden swing and pots of red geraniums made it a place I'd like to sit on warm summer nights and listen to the cicadas in the pine trees.

A curving brick walk led to the broad front steps and branched to a gate in a privacy fence that enclosed the side yard. Voices and an occasional burst of laughter floated over the fence from the back of the house.

I rang the front doorbell and, when no one answered, walked through the side gate to the backyard. A crowd of about twenty people mingled in small groups on a series of terraced wooden decks and bricked patios that filled the yard beneath the extensive canopy of an ancient live oak.

A long table held platters of food and a frosted cake with pink sugar roses and a fat numeral one candle. Beside the table, a galvanized tub filled with crushed ice cooled beer and sodas.

Adler stood over a charcoal grill, turning hamburgers. The fire ruddied his face, and he wore an orange-checkered apron with "Who invited all these tacky people?" inscribed in bold black letters.

"Hey, Skerritt." Steve Johnson called from behind the buffet table. "Figured out who's slaughtering the stock at the fat farm?"

"Not yet. But if you eat that mountain of potato salad on your plate, I may be adding you to the list of victims."

"Steve, watch these." Adler handed him the spatula and hurried toward me. "Glad you could make it. Come meet the birthday girl."

He led me to a group seated in Adirondack chairs at the base of the oak. A young woman with a child in her arms rose to greet me.

"Detective—Maggie," Adler said, "my wife, Sharon, and Jessica."

I caught only a fleeting impression of Sharon's green

eyes and dark brown hair before the youngster reached out her arms to me. Jessica was dressed in a white ruffled sunsuit and a broad-brimmed white hat turned up above her face. Dimples marked plump knees, elbows and rosy cheeks. She waved her arms, pumped her feet and laughed with a gurgling sound. The sight made my heart ache with a strange longing.

"You must be special," Sharon said. "She's been clinging to me since the party began. Won't even go to her grandparents."

"Hi, Jessica." I took the child, and she wrapped her chubby arms around my neck. Her red-gold curls brushed my nose, and she smelled of powder and that fresh, wholesome scent distinctive to babies and small children.

"Happy birthday, sweetie. I brought you a present." I sat in a nearby chair with the child in my lap and watched her shred wrapping paper. She grabbed the book upside down.

"Thank you," Sharon said. "I know how busy you've been." She knelt beside the chair and helped Jessica turn the pages. Her husband joined us.

"It's nothing—"

"Not just for the book," she said, "but for not giving Dave grief about the party. It would have been a shame for him to miss it."

I glanced around the group of relaxed and happy partygoers. "Enjoy it while you can, Adler," I said to Dave. "I've turned up another suspect."

"Tillett?" he asked.

"Maybe. And a lab technician Tillett fired a couple weeks ago, guy named Brent Dorman. Seems he has a special dislike for heavy people."

"Can't say I blame him. I like 'em slim myself." He nudged Sharon's slender hip with the toe of his Reebok.

"We'll all be fat and fifty someday," Sharon said, "if we live right." She picked up Jessica, who'd begun to fidget in my lap. "We're ready to cut the cake. Will you have some?"

I shook my head. "I have interviews to squeeze in before the day's over."

Adler walked me to my car. "Sorry you can't stay. I'll be back at the station before dark."

"Locate Brent Dorman for me. I want to question him as soon as possible."

I drove away as fast as I could without breaking the limit, trying to escape the awareness of things lost, the children I'd never had, the grandchildren I'd never hold. I cursed my own sentimentality, a useless emotion when it came to catching killers.

* * *

Five minutes later, I parked in front of Karen Englewood's house. The jalousie windows of the Florida room were cranked open, and voices flowed from the room. The conversation wasn't friendly. I sat in my car, more from a reluctance to interfere than a desire to eavesdrop. But I left my window down.

"Why can't you tell me where you've been since Friday?" Karen was shouting.

"Why don't you leave me the hell alone?" a male voice answered. "I'm not a kid anymore."

"You live in my house and I pay your bills. An explanation of your comings and goings is little enough to ask in return."

"Stuff it, Mom. You care more about those blimps you call clients than your own son. As far as I'm concerned, they can all rot in hell. Who needs the fat freaks?"

A loud crash yanked me from the car and propelled me up the front walk. The door flew open, and a tall young man, dressed in black jeans and a dark T-shirt embossed with scarlet dragons, almost knocked me down as he raced to the curb. Karen stood in the doorway and watched him go. He climbed into a faded Trans Am, revved the engine and scratched off down the street, leaving the smell of burning rubber hanging in the air.

"You okay?" I asked.

Tears tracked her cheeks, but she showed no sign of injury. She nodded and stepped aside. "Come in, Detective. I've given the neighbors enough of a show for one afternoon."

I followed her into the Florida room. Miniblinds had been partly closed against the late afternoon sun, plunging the room into shadow. I avoided shards of pottery and clumps of dirt and leaves from a broken urn near the door and sat in the wicker rocker. "Was that your son?"

"Yes, Larry. Every conversation I have with him is a battle." She pulled tissues from a box on an end table, wiped her eyes and blew her nose. "And me a psychologist."

"Hard to stay objective when it's your own kid."

"Tell me about it." She attempted a smile. "Larry's nineteen, and he's never forgiven me for divorcing his father four years ago. Running with the wrong crowd is his way of getting back at me."

She'd opened a door, so I plunged through it. "So you weren't at home by yourself Friday night?"

Her eyes widened. "You're good, Detective. How did you know?"

"Body language. You're not a good liar."

"Thank God for that." She laughed, but her features reverted quickly to sadness. "Larry and I had a huge fight Friday afternoon. He'd come home early from work and I guessed correctly that he'd been fired. When I questioned him about it, he blew up at me."

"Why did you suspect he'd been fired?"

"He'd been warned before about coming in late, hungover." She picked up her embroidery frame from the basket at her feet. "Larry's been mostly a loner since Jack and I split up, but sometimes he hangs with a crowd that gathers on one of the spoil islands off Pelican Point. They drink beer. And smoke pot. His clothes reek of it."

"I know that group. We've alerted the marine patrol, but it's hard to sneak up on a small island undetected. They toss the dope into the campfires. We arrested a few on drunk and disorderly charges."

"Larry was one of them. I've had to bail him out a few times. But he never seems to learn his lesson." She set aside her cloth without taking a stitch. "Who am I trying to kid? He isn't going to change."

"He's still young—"

"He's acting out, doing everything he can to lash out at me."

"Everything? Including killing your clients?"

"No!" Her hands shook, and she rammed them into the pockets of her skirt. "His actions are irritating, antisocial, but he'd never hurt anyone."

She didn't sound convinced.

"Where were you really Friday evening?" I asked.

"Driving. I went all over town looking for Larry. He'd left the house in such a mean and angry mood. I was afraid he might hurt…"

"Someone?"

"Himself." She spoke firmly, but whether to persuade herself or me, I couldn't tell. "I couldn't find him. He was gone all weekend until an hour ago, but he wouldn't tell me where he's been or what he's been up to."

Karen opened the blinds, and the sky flamed like the pulp of ripe mangoes above the setting sun. "Any idea," she asked, "who killed Edith and Sophia?"

Her change of subject was obvious, but it suited my purposes. "I need information. That's why I'm here."

"Have supper with me. I have a casserole in the oven, and Larry won't be back to share it."

I could never resist someone else's cooking. I followed the patter of her espadrilles down a dark hallway to the kitchen. It stretched across the back of the house and looked like a television soundstage for the Galloping Gourmet. Copper pans and strings of garlic hung from a rack above the stove, and a herb garden flourished in a bay window above the sink. The aroma of roasting chicken made my mouth water.

We ate at a scrubbed wooden table decorated with checkered place mats and terra-cotta pots of gerbera daisies. Karen served a salad of romaine and radicchio and dished up huge portions of chicken, brown rice and water chestnuts in a savory sauce. Savory—that's what my frozen packages always claimed. I didn't know sage from sassafras.

I took a bite of chicken, chewed and nodded my approval. "How long have you worked with Richard Tillett?"

"Ten years, since the clinic opened." She added artificial sweetener to her iced tea. "Best job I've ever had."

"Why's that?"

"Richard Tillett. He knows medicine and has compassion, too, a scarce commodity in too many doctors today."

I wondered if Tillett's bedside manner had played a part in Karen's divorce. "Is he the kind of man to benefit from another's misfortune?"

"I'm not sure what you mean."

"Are you aware of any money problems?"

Her face scrunched in thought as she toyed with her salad. "Our pay was late a few weeks ago, but he explained it as a temporary cash-flow problem. Lord, we've all had those, haven't we?"

"Tell me about Brent Dorman."

Anger flashed in her deep brown eyes. "A pompous ass."

I choked on my iced tea. "Liked him that much, eh?"

She picked up her knife and fork and attacked the romaine, shredding it into minute pieces. "Why he ever applied for work at the clinic, I'll never know. He hates overweight people with a passion."

"Passion enough to kill?"

She considered my question for a moment before answering. "No, he doesn't have the guts for anything so decisive. His hatred of heavy people is a way of making himself seem important, superior."

"What's more superior than the power of life and death?"

"Are Dr. Tillett and Brent suspects?"

"I have to investigate every angle."

"And you're concentrating on the clinic?"

"It's more than coincidence that Edith and Sophia belonged to the same group." Ignoring my yearning taste buds and remembering departmental weight standards, I declined her offer of more casserole.

"Only a psychopath," she said, "could murder so cold-bloodedly. And none of the staff or patients is psychopathic. I'd stake my credentials on that."

"Not even Brent Dorman?"

"Obsessive-compulsive maybe, but not psychopathic." She folded her arms on the tabletop and leaned toward me. "There's a crazy person out there killing fat people—"

"But Sophia wasn't fat."

"She was about ten to fifteen pounds overweight. To someone who hates fat enough to kill, even an extra ounce is probably too much. He'd view body weight the way an anorexic does—only emaciation is beautiful."

"Sounds like an overview of American culture." I shifted in my chair, cognizant of my sturdy thighs. "Models to movie stars."

"People have been murdered simply because their skin's the wrong color or they belong to the wrong ethnic or religious group. Why's it so hard to believe someone could be killed only because she's fat?" Karen insisted.

"It's not impossible," I conceded, "but it's a stretch."

She shook her head. "Obese people are one of the most maligned and abused groups in this country. Lots of people think nothing of taunting and insulting them openly. Some not only dislike them, they have a pathological fear of them, afraid that with too many chips or desserts or whatever they're tempted to binge on, they'll become fat, too. To them obese people represent what they fear most. And fear often leads to hatred."

Karen's eyes glittered in the soft light. She stood and removed the plates from the table. "There's a homicidal maniac roaming out there somewhere. You have to find this person, Detective, before he—or she—kills again."

CHAPTER 8

Iridescent slicks of oil glistened on the undulating surface of the marina basin, reflecting the orange sodium lights that flooded the area with perpetual daylight. Brine and fish odors floated on the wind. My footsteps on the weathered boards of the dock beat a muffled counterpoint to the water lapping against the pilings. I pulled my jacket closer against the chill that had descended with the sunset.

When I reached the far end of the dock, soft light escaped around the edges of the drawn curtains of the *Ten-Ninety-Eight*. It wasn't too late to turn back, to spare Bill the details of my case. He'd earned his freedom from such matters. Nowadays, his toughest decision was which televised sporting event to watch on Sunday afternoons.

But I didn't want to go home to my lonely condo, where the faces of Edith Wainwright and Sophia Morelli would haunt me. I stepped down to the walk that ran the length of his boat, pulled the vessel toward me with a mooring line and rapped on the cabin window.

Bill slid open the glass door to the rear deck and grinned up at me. "Look what the cat dragged in."

"Permission to come aboard?"

He reached out and steadied me as I maneuvered from the walk to the ice chest that doubled as a bench and down to the deck. His callused palms warmed my cold hands.

In the tiny cabin, the closed curtains created a snug nest. I kicked off my shoes and curled into a corner of the overstuffed loveseat that spanned the length of the lounge area. Characters conversed silently on the muted television that sat on a counter between the lounge and the galley.

Bill picked up the TV remote and killed the power.

"Don't let me interrupt your program," I said.

"I fell asleep during *Sixty Minutes*..." His voice trailed away as he rummaged beneath the counter in the galley and came up with two icy bottles of Michelob. He twisted off the tops and filled two pilsner glasses.

I settled deeper into the cushions and let the gentle motion of the boat rock me. Two murders within forty-eight hours had me wound tighter than a kid's toy, and it would take more than a beer to relax me. I doubted a sledgehammer would do the job.

Bill handed me a glass and placed a bowl of salted nuts on the cushion between us. "I heard about the Morelli murder on the radio. You've had a helluva weekend."

"That's not the half of it." I sipped the chilled brew and nibbled peanuts, trying not to count calories or fat grams.

He studied my face with a piercing look. "Your mother?"

"How'd you guess?"

"Whenever you two have it out, you get these tight little lines around the corners of your mouth. Like a lockjaw victim." He reached over and stroked my face with his thumb and index finger, making me smile.

"Probably psychological. I tighten up to keep from telling her off."

He grinned back. "Tell her off. It might do you good."

"I'd only create more tension. Besides, she's as frustrated with our relationship as I am. She probably thinks I'm a changeling, switched at birth, and that somewhere in the world, a perfect daughter who does all the right things—wears the right clothes, attends the proper parties, marries the perfect man—is pining for her real mother."

"Sounds like your sister."

His perception had made him an excellent investigator. "At least Caroline followed the script—married a socially prominent wealthy man, had two exemplary children who've provided Mother with four perfect great-grandchildren. Caroline's even chairing the art show this year to raise money for Mother's favorite charity—"

"Margaret, if you clutch that glass any tighter, it's going to shatter in your hand."

I released my death grip on the pilsner glass. "Mother's been this way all my life, so why is she driving me crazy now?"

"Maybe because you've got a double homicide on your hands?" He massaged the back of my neck.

Lured by those hands and his exceptional culinary skills, I could settle for a life with Bill. The million-dollar question was whether he'd want me. I'd assumed his proposals had been made in jest, but I was too afraid to ask, so I'd probably never know.

"I've had homicides before. But now I'm staring down the barrel of age fifty and realizing Mother—and I—are never going to change."

Bill moved the bowl of peanuts and pulled me closer. "You abandoned her world when you signed up for the academy. She can't begin to understand what your life is like. Don't hold it against her."

"You're right. Even though she's thirty-four years older than me, she's never worked a fatal traffic accident or had to deal with murder." I snuggled back against his broad chest. "Only another cop can truly understand what we deal with day to day."

"Remember Fernandez, who worked homicide in Tampa?"

I nodded. Fernandez had retired early with posttraumatic stress disorder. He'd begun waking in the middle of the night to find the victims from his cases sitting at the foot of his bed, demanding to know if he'd caught their killers. None of us had asked whether or not six years of retirement had banished the ghosts. We were afraid to know.

"How about a walk?" Bill said. "I've been a couch potato all day."

He tugged on a windbreaker, locked up the boat and hoisted me to the dock. We entered the park that bordered the marina and turned south on the path that paralleled the waterfront.

"The scuzzballs are out already." Bill nodded toward

a bearded man, dressed in faded army fatigues and leaning against the wall of the public rest rooms.

I recognized Lenny Jacobs, working undercover vice, but gave no sign of acknowledgment. I didn't know who might be watching.

We strolled along the bay, watched the night herons skitter among the tidal flats, and listened to the calls of screech owls and a chuck-will's-widow. An ambulance passed, lights flashing and siren silent, headed for Clearwater. Except for an occasional jogger and a couple walking their dog, we were alone in the night. I brought Bill up to speed on all that had happened since our supper at Frenchy's the night before. It seemed like weeks ago.

When we reached the mouth of Stevenson Creek where it emptied into the sound, we turned back toward Pelican Bay and chose a bench beneath a massive cedar, its trunk gnarled and twisted by the onshore winds. Across the sound, the lights of Clearwater and Pelican Beaches twinkled like a Christmas display.

"When I talked with Karen Englewood tonight," I said, "she seemed convinced we're dealing with a psychopathic killer, but I can't tell whether she really believes that or is trying to divert attention from her son."

"You've just given me the facts, ma'am," Bill said in his Joe Friday voice. "What do your instincts tell you?"

"That everyone I've talked to is hiding something. That the killer could be any one of them or some faceless psycho working in a vitamin factory in Ohio."

"Didn't you say that Mick Rafferty came up empty on the vitamins?"

"He only had time this afternoon to check the pills collected from Morelli and the five surviving group members. All tested clean. I'll know tomorrow about the other vitamins from Tillett's office."

"Anyone working this case besides you and Adler?"

I kicked a pinecone from beneath the bench and sent it twirling down the bluff into a tidal pool. "Shelton had already cut CID by two detectives before Carter moved to Memphis. Now Adler and I make up the entire division. Not that I have any love for Shelton, but it's not his fault. The city council's looking for ways to save money. They've been on his back to cut costs."

Bill uttered a string of curses that would have sent my hoity-toity mother into cardiac arrest. "Those number crunchers can't tell their asses from holes in the ground. Almost every other community in the country is pumping up police presence and initiating community policing to reduce crime and guard against terrorism, and these pinheads want to cut our police force?"

"It looks good on paper and saves them from raising taxes, the ultimate in political self-preservation."

"God, what idiots."

I sat back and enjoyed the spectacle of Bill Malcolm in a rage. I'd seen the awe-inspiring display only twice before, the first time when Tricia divorced him, the second when I left the Tampa PD for Pelican Bay.

His anger ebbed as he exhausted his earthy vocabulary. "How do you expect to solve homicides with only you and Adler on this case, not to mention the rest of your caseload?"

I shrugged. "I'll do the best I can. What choice do I have?"

"Let me help."

Bill had been one of the best homicide detectives in the Tampa department. But there'd been a time when I'd wondered if he'd reach retirement or a nervous breakdown first. Retirement had won, and I didn't want to place him back on the firing line. "I don't know—"

He grasped my shoulders and twisted me to face him. Moonlight lit the planes of his face and highlighted the stubborn set of his jaw. "You said you're afraid the killer may strike again, that there're five more at risk in the group from the clinic. At least let me drive to Boca Raton and check out Tillett's alibi."

The darkness couldn't hide the glint in his eyes or the eagerness in his voice, a sign of the same love/hate of police work that I felt myself.

"God knows, I can use the help with Boca," I admitted. "But I'm not committing to anything more. Understood?"

He rose and pulled me to my feet. "Perfectly. Commitment of any kind has always scared the crap out of you."

His words hit closer to home than I cared to admit. I wanted commitment but was terrified it wouldn't take. "We're such good friends. Why spoil that friendship by making a commitment out of it?"

With a sigh of frustration, he shook his head and changed the subject. "I'll leave for the East Coast tonight."

I had to run to keep up with him all the way back to the marina.

Bill had been in Boca for hours when I reached my office at seven-thirty the next morning. I'd had one beer and six hours' sleep the night before, but my body insisted I'd been on a four-day binge. Stiff and sore, with eyelids like sandpaper, I pitied the first person to cross my path.

Adler caught the brunt. He bounded into the office as energized as if he'd come off three weeks' leave. "Thanks for stopping by yesterday. Jessica loves her book. I've read it to her so many times, I've memorized it."

"What have you got on Wainwright?"

He recoiled at the snap in my voice, and a flush darkened his face and the tips of his ears. "I located her only surviving relative, a ninety-year-old uncle in a nursing home in Michigan."

"Whoa, the kid was only twenty-two. How can she have an uncle who's ninety?"

"A great-uncle. She was raised by her grandparents. Her parents died in a plane crash in Chicago in 1989, and Edith came here to live."

"What about a will?"

"Haven't located one yet, but even if I do, the uncle says there're no assets. Edith had to mortgage the house to pay the old couple's medical bills and to bury them."

Orphaned, socially outcast by her obesity, poor, and now murdered. Nobody deserved all that. The skin on the backs of my hands and my upper arms itched angrily. I'd be soaking in oatmeal baths before this case was closed.

"Bill Malcolm's gone to Boca to check out Tillett's alibi," I said.

"Oh, yeah?" There were a thousand questions in his eyes, but none I wanted to answer.

"He misses the job," I said in my most neutral voice. "Likes to keep his hand in now and then."

Adler nodded with a look that said he knew I was sidestepping. He sat in the chair behind what had been Carter's desk and locked his fingers behind his head. "I've got a funny feeling about Tillett."

"Everyone connected to this case gives me a funny feeling." I dug my hands into my pockets to keep from scratching.

"Tillett has motive for Sophia's murders," Adler said. "A million big ones, and opportunity, through access to the vitamin supplies. If his alibi doesn't hold up—"

"Don't get ahead of yourself." The irritation in my skin transferred to my voice. "Let's wait for Bill's report. Have you located Dorman?"

Adler stood and ripped a page off the notepad on the desk. "I'm on my way now to check out his last known address."

"I'll need your help at five today with the interviews

of Tillett's staff and patients. You can meet me at his clinic."

"Sure." He paused in the doorway. "While you're there, maybe the doctor can give you something for that rash."

He circled his face with his finger and pointed toward me before taking off.

I jumped from my chair with the alacrity of a much younger woman and sprinted down the hall to the rest room. The mirror confirmed Adler's observation. Angry red blotches covered my face. I shoved up my sleeves. My arms were enveloped in spots as well. A persistent itching beneath my panty hose confirmed the welts had spread to my legs.

Cold compresses of the department's industrial-strength paper towels eased the inflammation on my face, but the rest of me was in agony, my worst eruption since right before I'd left the Tampa department.

I'd visited a dermatologist then, convinced I'd contracted some rare exotic disease while patrolling the docks of the Port of Tampa. The doctor had assured me it was only hives, probably stress-related. He'd been right about the stress. Three young girls under the age of twelve had been murdered in the city that year, and the entire department was on alert. Two years later, the killer was still on the loose, and I'd decided I'd had enough of murder. That's when I decided to transfer to the small-town department of Pelican Bay to lessen my chances of having to deal with homicides.

I suppressed a grunt of disgust. I could run from murder but I couldn't hide.

I returned to my desk, scrawled an address from my files and hurried to my car. At the Apothecary Shop—a common drugstore in Pelican Bay's chic antiques district would be heresy—I bought calamine lotion and Benadryl. A female pharmacist in her early twenties rang up my purchases.

"Wow." She shoved her chewing gum to one cheek to speak. "That's the worst case of urticaria I've seen."

She hadn't lived long enough to see much.

"Thanks," I said. "It's worse than it looks."

At home, I stripped off black gabardine slacks and a red silk blouse and slathered calamine lotion over my face and body, dressed again minus panty hose, and gulped down a megadose of Benadryl. The agony had eased slightly by the time I'd climbed back into my car and turned toward Clearwater.

The changes in the town depressed me. Once a bustling little city with a beautiful waterfront, its downtown had withered for years.

I parked on a side street and entered a mostly deserted building. On the third floor, I traveled a dark hallway to an office that overlooked the alley. Facts, Inc., was the brainchild of Archer Phillips, an old high school classmate of mine. Archer, the Mario Andretti of the information superhighway, had turned his computer skills into a thriving business that searched records of all kinds, primarily for insurance companies and private investigators.

The Pelican Bay PD seldom used his services. Complete background checks on individuals ran as high as a couple of thousand dollars, and the department was too strapped to lay out that kind of cash. What Archer could locate in days would take a couple of detectives months to uncover. I couldn't wait months.

I resisted the urge to rake my nails down my itching arms for quick relief before opening the door. Not only did I hope to avoid further deaths by bringing these latest cases to a close quickly; in a very literal way, I was saving my own skin.

A desiccated little woman with thinning gray hair pulled back in a knot sat behind the reception desk. She studied me over the gold wire frames of her glasses. "Margaret Skerritt, I almost didn't recognize you. My, how you've changed."

"Age does that to us all, Mrs. Phillips. Is Archer in?"

"Yes…"

I could see the wheels turning behind her watery eyes and sensed her dilemma. She was wondering which would be worse for her beloved son, an official visit from law enforcement or a personal one from an unmarried former classmate. Archer had spent almost fifty years under his mother's thumb. I found a small degree of comfort in the fact that someone's relationship with his mother was worse than mine.

"Can I tell him what this is about?"

"Sure. I need information."

She hesitated as if wanting to ask more, then shrugged her bony shoulders and disappeared through a door behind her desk. When she returned, Archer followed her.

"Margaret, good to see you!"

Archer's greeting was too hearty, and he almost tripped on his small feet in his hurry to usher me into his office and close the door. He motioned me toward a chair in front of his desk and settled his pear-shaped bulk behind it. He forced his thick lips into a smile, and I wondered if the genetic marker for genius carried ugliness as well.

"What's this all about?" Apprehension glittered in his tiny eyes.

"I have two potential homicide suspects. I need the works on them. ASAP. Employment history, assets and liabilities, criminal and driving records, anything you can find."

"That's what I do best." He smoothed his pink guayabera over his paunch, then punched the keys on his desk calculator. "I figure about fifteen hundred apiece. Do I bill the department?"

"No bill. I'm calling in my debt."

"That's blackmail—"

The door to the outer office swung open, and Mrs. Phillips entered with a tray. She placed it on Archer's desk and handed me coffee in a dainty cup and saucer. "Did you say blackmail?" she asked.

I accepted the sugar bowl she offered and stirred in three mounds from a silver spoon. Archer's cup rattled in its saucer. He'd begun to sweat.

"Sorry," I said. "Police business. It's confidential."

When she'd returned to the front office and closed the door, he slammed his cup and saucer on the desktop, sloshing coffee over the papers scattered there. "You can't do this, Margaret."

I gritted my teeth. Pushing people around wasn't my idea of a good time, but I needed information fast.

"I have a list of seven people. Two on that list have already been murdered. If my partner and I have to gather the facts we need, the other five may be dead before we're finished."

"But I can't afford—"

"You can afford that condo in Pelican Bay, a nice little love nest I'm sure your mama has no knowledge of. I'd hate to disillusion her about her devoted Archer."

I'd stumbled across Archer's condo and his regular visits to the woman who lived there during the stakeout of a drug dealer two years ago. When Archer spotted me, he'd begged me never to say anything to his mother. I'd agreed, with the stipulation that he might return the favor by providing information for me in the future.

He pulled a large handkerchief from the pocket of his polyester slacks and ran it over his perspiring bald dome. "You can't tell her. Her heart, it could kill her."

Mrs. Phillips had the look of a woman who might live forever, but I had no intention of revealing Archer's secret life. The poor guy deserved whatever pleasure he could get. And I deserved a break on this case.

"Just get me the information I need." I wrote Richard Tillett and Lester Morelli on my notepad, ripped off the top sheet and handed it across the desk. "You can donate your fee to the department and deduct it from your income tax."

"It'll take some time."

"Time is something I don't have. I'll check with you at the end of the week."

His glance darted around the office as if searching for an excuse. "I may be out of town."

"Then I'll check with your mother."

"No!" He crumpled in his chair like an inflatable doll with an air leak. "I'll have what you need by Friday afternoon."

"Margaret," Mrs. Phillips called to me in a stage whisper as I left his office.

"Yes?"

"You really must do something about your makeup."

I touched my face where the calamine lotion had dried in a scaly residue. "It's not—"

"You're right, it's not your color at all. Makes you look bilious. You'll never catch a man looking like that."

I grinned and the dried calamine cracked. "I'm like the Mounties. I always get my man."

I had a catch to make, all right, but whether it was a man or a woman remained to be seen.

CHAPTER 9

Ted Trask, Lester Morelli's neighbor, met me in the lobby of the SunTrust building on Pelican Bay's Main Street. As Estelle, my mother's housekeeper of my childhood, would have said, he was a tall drink of water, over six feet tall, lean and tanned with the look of money stamped all over his dark suit and yellow silk tie. We rode the elevator to the third-floor offices of Trask, Farmingham and Lane.

I stifled a yawn, a combination of too little sleep and too much Benadryl. "What's your firm's specialty?"

"Our partners and associates work in all aspects of the law."

"Must add up to a lot of billable hours."

He chuckled and perfect white teeth contrasted with his tanned complexion. "Between reruns of *The Practice* and John Grisham novels, we lawyers have no secrets anymore."

The bell dinged discreetly and the elevator doors whispered open. He stood aside for me to exit into the reception area. A secretary, who looked remarkably like Mrs. Doubtfire, glanced up.

"Hold my calls, please, Eudora." Trask led the way through a central room lined with law books to his corner office. Glass walls provided a panoramic view of the waterfront.

I sat on a soft leather chair and fought the urge to fall asleep. "As I told you on the phone, I'm investigating the murder of Sophia Morelli."

Trask sat at his desk, a slab of black marble on two massive glass columns, and fiddled with an onyx-handled letter opener. "Murder's something usually reserved for the news. When it happens next door, it's a shock. And when it's a woman like Sophia, it's a real tragedy."

"Have you known the Morellis long?"

"Our house was the first one built on the point. About five years ago, right before Les and Sophia married, they started their house next door."

"What can you tell me about Sophia?"

Trask leaned back and balanced the letter opener on one finger. "Quiet. Sweet."

"That's it?"

"When they first moved in, Sophia's poor health kept her practically bedridden. She spent most of her time in her morning room, sleeping, reading or just watching the water."

"But her health improved after she lost weight. Didn't her behavior change then?"

Trask looked thoughtful. "No. But Sophia was always shy. We just assumed she preferred her own company."

"We?"

"Janet, my wife, and I."

"So Janet and Sophia weren't friends?"

"Janet is hyperactive, the opposite of Sophia. She's involved in a dozen charities, plus the activities of our three children. She hardly ever saw Sophia, except to wave to her from the car."

Janet's similarity to my sister, Caroline, sent the nerve endings in my skin into spasms again. "How would you describe the Morelli marriage?"

"Les is…was devoted to her. Waited on her hand and foot, when he wasn't working at the restaurant. And even though she'd begun to feel better, he worried about her constantly."

"Did they ever quarrel?"

"Are you married, Detective Skerritt?"

I flushed under my calamine mask. "No."

"Every married couple quarrels. Those who say they don't are either lying or have given up on making their marriage work."

"And the Morellis?"

"I heard them raise their voices at each other a few times, but never in my presence, so I can't tell you what they argued about. Probably the usual things."

"Such as?"

"How much time he spent at work, how she wouldn't take care of herself the way he wanted her to, money—"

"Are you speculating?"

Trask shook his head. "I've been Les's doubles partner for years and consider myself his friend. He's confided in me. I'm telling you this now only to demonstrate how much Sophia meant to him."

"Telling me what?"

"What they fought over. Sophia wanted to hire someone else to manage the restaurant."

"Didn't Lester do his job?"

"Too well. It kept him away from home day and night. But he refused to give it up. Said he didn't want people to think he'd married Sophia for her money. He wanted to earn his way."

"So he neglected his wife for the business?"

Trask raised an eyebrow. "Have you ever thought of going into criminal law? You do a hell of a cross-examination."

And he'd done a hell of a sidestep. "Did Lester Morelli neglect his wife?"

Trask rose to his feet and adjusted the gold-and-diamond links in his French cuffs. "Les devoted every minute he wasn't at the restaurant to Sophia, driving her to the clinic, having all their meals delivered from the restaurant so she didn't have to cook or be bothered by servants in the house. He'd sit for hours with her when she wasn't well. If you think he killed his wife, you're way off base. The guy adored her."

Lester Morelli sounded too good to be true. "Did you notice anyone or anything out of the ordinary on your street this past weekend? Particularly anyone around the Morelli place?"

Trask circled his desk and began moving toward the door, an unsubtle way of ending our interview. "There was a delivery from the restaurant Saturday night. I remember seeing the logo on the van."

I rose and headed for the door.

"Wait," Trask said. "There was something else. Saturday morning."

"What?"

"Early Saturday about six, I awakened early and was having coffee on my deck. Watching the sunrise."

My body screamed for more Benadryl, and I struggled to keep the impatience from my voice. "What did you see?"

"A boat anchored off the Morellis' beach, a small outboard. Two young men were walking along the shore. I started inside to call Security, but they saw me, waded to their boat and took off."

"Can you describe them?"

"Late teens, early twenties. Long-haired, tall, slender. Dressed in dark jeans, dark T-shirts."

"And the boat?"

"White, no identifying marks."

"Which way did they go?"

"Once they'd headed west toward the channel, I didn't pay much attention."

"Thanks. I appreciate your help."

I hurried through the law library and the reception area and onto a deserted elevator, then allowed myself the luxury of scratching all the way to the first floor.

The parking lot of the weight-management clinic was full when I arrived a little before five o'clock, and I finally found a space at the hospital across the street.

The clear October weather had turned muggy, and as I trekked toward the clinic, the humidity turned the calamine into a thin paste that coated my body.

I planned to go straight to the yacht club from the clinic, so I wore the navy linen dress and jacket I usually reserved for court appearances. I wobbled in the unaccustomed height of my matching pumps, insecure in the knowledge that no matter how I dressed, I'd look like a bag lady beside the sartorial elegance of Caroline and my mother. I bought clothes only once every other year, but my sister lived to shop. Cutting off her credit cards would be like switching off her oxygen. Sometimes I wanted to do both.

Adler leaned against his car by the clinic entrance, waiting for me. He cut loose a wolf whistle as I approached. "Looking good, Detective Skerritt."

"Save your observations for the folks inside." The minute I spoke, I regretted my snappishness.

"Yes, ma'am."

"And don't call me ma'am."

He beat me to the door and started to tug it open. I laid a restraining hand on his arm. "Sorry. I didn't mean to bite your head off."

He shrugged, smiled and squinted his brown eyes.

"These murders have us both on edge. No wonder you're...prickly."

I resisted the urge to smack the grin off his face. "This clinic holds the link that connects the dead women. Let's see if we can wrap this up."

He pulled the door open, then followed me into the waiting room. The people inside fell silent at the sight of us. I had time for little more than a fleeting impression of five large bodies with upturned faces before Karen Englewood ushered us into the inner office.

"Officer Adler can use my office," she said, "and Detective Skerritt, you can use Dr. Tillett's. I'll send each patient to you as soon as Dr. Tillett has seen them."

"And the staff?" I asked.

"Gale Whatley's waiting for you, the door on the left at the end of the hall."

Tillett's office told me little about the man. The decor was functional and unremarkable with none of the pretentiousness of Ted Trask's place. Stacks of files and papers covered every surface, except for a few square feet of the credenza behind his desk that displayed pictures of Stephanie, the small boy I'd seen at their house and an older girl whom I guessed to be their daughter. Built-in bookcases housed a wall of medical texts and journals.

The doctor's office manager sat on a love seat and picked at the cuticles of her peach-lacquered nails. When I closed the door behind me, she jumped, and color stained her prominent cheekbones. In her late twenties, she had the lean body of a fashion model, looking in desperate need of a good hot meal just to stay alive. Tillett's obese patients probably ground their teeth at the sight of her.

Long, dark hair billowed around her flawless face, and her gray eyes reflected the panicked look of a wild animal caught in headlights. Being interrogated by the police has that effect on people, even those with nothing to hide.

"God, this is awful," Gale said. "Do you have any idea who's doing it?"

"We have a few suspects but no one in custody at this time." I rejected the chair behind the desk for one across from her. "That's why I need your help."

"Me?" She laced her fingers in her lap. "I don't know anything about the murders. Just what I've heard from Karen and the news reports."

"I'm hoping you can fill in background information."
She stared at me. "Like what?"

"What can you tell me about Edith and Sophia?"

"Not much." Her expression softened, and she unclenched her fingers. "Both were very reserved. I spoke with them only when they paid their bills."

"Did you observe their interactions with others in the group or with Mrs. Englewood?"

"Look, I sit at my desk and collect fees and dispense vitamins and diet-drink mix, so I usually see only one patient at a time."

"So the victims never had problems with any other members?"

"I wouldn't call it a problem, exactly." With a jerky movement, she flipped her hair off her face.

"Tell me about it." The social taboo against snitching runs deep in our society. Digging out facts was worse than pulling teeth.

"One of the patients is…difficult. He complains about everything. He's faulted everybody for not taking turns, for hogging the discussion, for lying about calorie intake and weight loss. He's accused me of overcharging him, Gina of purposely hurting him when she draws blood, and Karen of not taking his complaints seriously."

"His name?"

"Peter Castleberry." Her gray eyes, accentuated by heavy liner, widened. "But he's not a killer. Peter's bristly attitude is a defense. He's been maligned all his life because of his weight, and he suffers constant pain and discomfort as well as insults. Anyone would be unpleasant under those circumstances."

My hives festered, and I recalled my treatment of Adler earlier. Surliness didn't necessarily produce homicidal tendencies, but I deferred judgment on Castleberry until I could talk with him myself. "How did he get along with Dr. Tillett?"

"A kind of love/hate relationship." She shifted on the sofa and crossed long legs encased in expensive stockings, reminding me of my own itchy limbs confined in panty hose that suddenly seemed too small. "Castleberry depends on the doctor to keep him alive, but he's a man with a man's ego. He hates that dependency."

I longed for a genuine bad guy, someone whose corruption stood out against the purity of those around him, like a giant arrow pointing to my killer. All I found were murky shades of gray, proving the complexities of the people I interrogated.

A nautical clock above the desk chimed the half hour.

"Just one more question, Ms. Whatley. Where were you between 5:00 and 7:00 p.m. Friday?"

She clasped her hands again in a white-knuckled

grip. "The office was closed Friday because of Dr. Tillett's seminar, so I left that morning and drove to Fort Myers to visit my sister. I didn't get back until last night."

Conveniently absent the entire weekend. "Ask Mrs. Englewood to send in the next person."

She stood and smoothed her short, form-fitting skirt over slender thighs. "I can give you my sister's number if—"

"I'll contact you if I need it."

After Gale Whatley left, Marilee Ginsberg maneuvered in on a Lark scooter. She explained that her arthritic knees had rebelled years ago against supporting her two-hundred-pound-plus bulk. But she couldn't tell me anything new about the victims or their interactions with the support group or staff.

In the hallway, Peter Castleberry's gasping breath announced his approach. He stomped into the room, lowered his four hundred pounds with a thud onto the loveseat, filling it almost entirely, and scowled at me with porcine eyes. If the thin supremacists ever needed a poster child for their hate campaign, Castleberry was a casting director's dream. Unlike Marilee Ginsberg, who looked like everyone's favorite grandmother, he inspired instant dislike.

"Why are you wasting my time when you should be out catching a killer?" His thin, reedy voice was a surprise coming from such a big man.

"Are you afraid of being questioned?" I could match him measure for measure at being obnoxious, a trait at which I'd become expert after twenty-two years of dealing with lowlifes.

His tortured intake of air hissed in the room. "I got nothing to hide."

"Good. Tell me about Edith and Sophia."

"Whiners, both of 'em. Always wanted to be the center of attention. And they were. Karen and Dr. T. always favored the women."

"Why was that?"

He shrugged. "Who knows? Life ain't fair. If it was, would I look like this?"

To describe Castleberry as hostile would have been a gross understatement. The man was mad at the world. But angry enough to kill? "Where were you between 5:00 and 7:00 p.m. Friday?"

"Where I always am, at home. Where's a guy like me going to go? On a hot date?" His bitter laughter dissolved into a wheezing cough.

"Can someone verify that you were at home?"

"I've lived alone for over twelve years, ever since my

loving mama called me a fat slob, told me to get a job and kicked me out."

"Did you get a job?"

He shook his head and his triple chins wobbled. "Only for a few months for a photography studio, but I've been on disability for years. Now I've lost a hundred pounds on Dr. Tillett's program, and when I've lost a hundred more, I plan to work as a photographer again."

Photography. If I remembered correctly, cyanide was a component used in developing film. But even if Castleberry had the means and motive for murder, did he have the physical stamina or agility to pull off the crimes? And wouldn't people have remembered a four-hundred-pound man if they'd seen him in the neighborhood? Castleberry was a viable suspect, but I couldn't make an arrest based merely on speculation.

Darkness had fallen when Adler walked me to my car, shortening his long-legged stride to keep pace with me. "I interviewed Rosco Fields and Charlene Jamison, both too ill and feeble to do much of anything, much less commit murder. I also talked to Naomi Calvin, the nurse, and Gina Peyton, the lab technician."

"Turn up anything interesting?"

"Just a few common threads. All, except Castleberry, think Tillett walks on water. No conflicts with him or among the victims, except for Castleberry, who fights with everybody. They all indicated the guy's about as cuddly as a porcupine."

My itching intensified with a vengeance. I dug a bottle of Benadryl capsules out of my pocket and swallowed two dry. Between the lack of progress in the case and my upcoming dinner with Mother, my skin had more eruptions than a Nostradamus prophecy. "Anything about Lester Morelli come up?"

"Solicitous. Everyone used the word to describe his devotion to his wife. She didn't drive, so he accompanied her to every appointment."

"We're back where we started." My feet ached in the unfamiliar high heels, and I longed to soak my itching skin in a warm bath. "Have you found Brent Dorman?"

"Moved. Left no forwarding address. Fields, Jamison and Calvin all complained how insulting he'd been. If I were a betting man I'd say our murderer is a toss-up between him and Tillett."

I climbed into my Volvo. "We'll know more about Tillett when Bill returns from Boca Raton. Keep after Dorman."

"Right after dinner with the women in my life." He

closed my door, gave a jaunty salute and sauntered back to his car.

I envied his youth and optimism, squelched a surge of maternal affection and braced myself to face Mother's displeasure as I headed toward the yacht club.

CHAPTER 10

When I pulled into the entrance of the yacht club, a teenage valet opened my car door. I tossed him my keys, grabbed the gift-wrapped book on the front seat and hurried inside. I was an hour late.

Twin Waterford chandeliers, suspended from the cathedral ceiling of the lobby, cast subdued lighting on the polished oak floors, Oriental carpets and a trestle table bearing a floral arrangement the size of a Volkswagen Bug. Whispers, discreet laughter and the muffled clink of sterling flatware against bone china drifted from the adjacent dining room.

A hatchet-faced hostess in black silk and pearls greeted me, and I suppressed the automatic reflex of flashing my badge. "Mrs. Skerritt's party, please."

She gave me a head-to-toe glance, and disapproval flicked across her heavily powdered face before she turned toward the dining room. "This way."

I followed her stiff back through the dimly lighted dining room and out double doors onto the terrace. I've faced homicidal maniacs, drug-crazed killers and reckless juveniles who'd as soon shoot a cop as breathe, but nothing unnerved me as much as these social elite, gussied up and gathered on their own turf. Their cool, sliding glances carried a punch heftier than a blow to the gut.

Worst of all was the same look in my mother's eyes. She watched me approach her table that overlooked sand dunes and moonlit Gulf on the terrace's far end. For eighty-two, the old girl looked fantastic—thick white hair pulled back by a black satin bow, and a white silk blouse with a Mandarin collar and flowing sleeves beneath a black tunic. The Queen of England couldn't have looked more elegant. Or more intimidating.

My father had been both bridge and buffer between my mother and me, but after his death, a chasm had opened, deep, wide and dangerous. The pinched look around her mouth told me it was going to be a rough evening.

"You're late, Margaret. We've already ordered." Diamond rings flashed on her slender fingers as she motioned to an empty seat opposite her at the round table, and I slid into it. The centerpiece of stargazer lilies, Mother's favorite, blocked me from her view.

A waiter appeared at my elbow, and I ordered a vodka and tonic and the catch of the day.

Caroline sat on Mother's right, composed and classy in an ecru designer dress that matched the ash-blond tones of her shoulder-length hair. Eight years my senior, Caroline was no more blond than I was, and only weekly trips to the hairdresser and liberal applications of L'Oréal produced the golden illusion.

On Mother's left, Caroline's stodgy husband, Huntington Yarborough, fawned over his mother-in-law. His insurance agency, the largest in Clearwater, produced the necessary income to support Caroline's expensive tastes. My niece, Michelle, a carbon copy of her mother, sipped champagne between her father and her husband, Chad, next to me.

"Where are the kids?" I whispered to him.

"Home with a sitter. Too solemn an occasion for strained peas or a colicky baby." He grinned, but his eyes reflected the agony of a fellow sufferer.

Mother shifted in her chair to eye me around the lilies. "Margaret, meet Cedric Langford. He rushed back from polo in West Palm just for my birthday."

The stranger on my left, athletic and tanned with

distinguished gray hair and the horse-faced looks of an aristocrat, spoke in clipped British tones. "Your mother's spoken often of you."

Experience told me Cedric was unattached and available and that Mother was matchmaking again. My skin protested with a new surge of misery. The Benadryl wasn't working. When the waiter placed my drink before me, I finished half of it in a gulp.

As the alcohol began its anesthetizing task, fragments of conversation floated around me.

"We've almost made it through another hurricane season," Hunt said.

"I'm not worried," Mother said. "I've lived here over seventy years without experiencing a major one. I doubt we'll be blown away in my lifetime."

"Mother, Hal Stowers has donated his latest painting for auction at the art show." Caroline's self-satisfied voice cut through the fog in my brain.

"Wonderful," Mother gushed. "You do know how to bring out the best, dear."

I tuned the chatter out. Nobody asked what I'd been doing, and I didn't volunteer. Mother didn't consider crime, especially murder, a fit topic for dinner conversation. I ate broiled snapper silently and sipped chardonnay. By the time the plates had been removed, I battled drooping lids and bit my lower lip to keep from yawning.

"Here's a little something from Hunt and me." Caroline presented Mother with a small box wrapped in silver paper. "Happy birthday, darling."

I'd poured over art books at Barnes & Noble and finally selected a coffee-table volume of Monet prints with accompanying color photographs of the places he'd painted. I nudged Chad and handed him the book to pass down the table. "Happy birthday, Mother."

Mother adored Monet, but as I watched her open Caroline's present, I again took a back seat to my sister.

"Sweetheart, how marvelous." Mother lifted a ruby-and-diamond pin in the shape of a lily from its velvet box and pinned it to her tunic. "It's perfect. Where did you find such a treasure?"

"St. Armand's Circle. You know how I love to shop there." Caroline beamed in triumph across the table.

"When the going gets tough, the tough go shopping," I muttered. I loved my sister, but I had about as much in common with her as a Samurai warrior. We might as well have been born on different planets.

Mother slit the tape on the William Morris wrapping and uncovered my gift. "How thoughtful, Margaret. Thank you."

She leafed briefly through a page or two and set it aside.

Caroline leaned toward Cedric. "Margaret loves books. She has her master's degree in library science."

"Are you a librarian?" Cedric asked.

I could tell his question sprang more from politeness than from interest, but I answered, anyway. "No, actually, I'm—"

"How absolutely gorgeous!" Mother clapped her hands with delight as the waiter carried in a tiered cake. So many candles encircled each layer, if we'd been inside, the smoke alarms would have sounded.

I finished the last of my wine while the others sang "Happy Birthday." I have a voice like a parrot being fried alive, and out of concern for the others, remained silent. I set down my glass, and the sounds around me ebbed as my eyelids closed.

"Margaret?" Mother's voice penetrated the darkness.

I awoke to discover my cheek pressed against the wool shoulder of Cedric's blazer. Too late I remembered the sedative effects of Benadryl mixed with alcohol. I sat up quickly and brushed without effect at the streak of calamine on Cedric's coat.

"Sorry, I've had a long day."

"Perhaps Cedric will drive you home, dear." Mother

smiled benevolently around the lilies. "Chad can follow in your car, and Michelle can pick him up at your place."

I'd played right into her matchmaking hands, so thoroughly I could see no way out. "We'll finish dessert first, Mother. I wouldn't dream of leaving your party early."

My Benadryl-befuddled brain churned sluggishly, searching for a way to rid myself of the handsome and eminently eligible polo player without offending him or my mother. I took tiny bites of cake in an attempt to delay the inevitable.

My procrastination was rewarded when the attractive young waiter leaned past me to fill Cedric's coffee cup, and I observed the deep, sultry look that passed between them. My very proper and ultraconservative mother would have a conniption fit if she learned she'd set me up with a gay man.

Cedric drove me home, but after walking me to the door, he sprinted back to his Ferrari, no doubt for a liaison with the yacht club waiter. Chad parked my Volvo in its reserved space beneath the carport and waved goodbye before climbing in with Michelle and taking off.

I started a pot of coffee brewing while I took a warm shower to soothe my skin, then dressed in jeans, a pullover and sneakers. I was clipping my badge and holster to my belt when my doorbell rang.

Bill Malcolm, looking dapper and delicious in a blue blazer, gray slacks and immaculate deck shoes, stood on my doorstep. He pointed to the gun on my belt. "You coming or going?"

"I was heading for the station, but I can wait. Come in."

"I just got in from Boca." He lifted his head and sniffed. "Do I smell coffee?"

"Fresh pot. Want some?"

He followed me into the kitchen and leaned against the counter while I filled two mugs.

"Why the fancy duds?" I asked. "A heavy date?"

"Most of the heavies around here are turning up dead." The skin around his blue eyes crinkled. "But the clothes did help me fit in at the Boca Resort. Do you have anything to eat in this seldom-used room allegedly called a kitchen?"

I tossed him a half-full bag of chocolate chip cookies. "Any luck in Boca?"

He strolled into my living room with the ease of a frequent visitor and folded his lanky frame into an armchair. "This case is really getting to you, isn't it?"

"It's just a case like any other murder case." I guzzled coffee, hoping the caffeine would counteract the effect of the booze and Benadryl.

"You don't fool me, Margaret. You haven't had hives like this since we went after that guy in Tampa who was icing kids and dumping their bodies in the bay. But even with that gunk on your face, you're still gorgeous."

I'd recently checked my bathroom mirror, but it wasn't polite to call him a liar to his face. "What about Tillett's alibi?"

Bill drew a small notebook from his inside coat pocket and flipped the pages. "I started with the airline. Tillett flew in and out of Boca when he said he did. On arrival, he took the resort's limousine from the airport. The desk clerk confirmed he checked in right before noon on Friday. Like the clerk told Adler, he remembered because the doctor raised a stink when his room wasn't ready."

"After that?"

"After that, we got a problem. I checked with maids, bellmen, concierge, desk clerks, the golf and tennis pros, Maintenance, you name it. No one remembered seeing Tillett leave his room or the hotel."

"Can anyone verify he was actually in his room the whole time?"

"Nope. You said Tillett swears he didn't leave his room from Friday noon until Saturday for the seminar's morning meeting, and I can't find anyone to contradict him, but—" He popped an entire cookie into his mouth and chewed.

I waited, trying not to scratch.

Bill washed the cookie down with coffee and examined his notes. "The clerk who checked him in said Tillett asked him to hold all his calls. The doctor collected his messages Saturday morning."

"That would fit," I said. "He claimed he went to Boca early to work on his speech, so he probably didn't want to be interrupted."

"Maybe. But I can't find any evidence he was there. He made no calls from the phone in his room, ordered nothing from room service, used nothing from the minibar."

"If Tillett came back to the West Coast, he'd probably have rented a car."

Bill nodded. "I checked out rental-car agencies, too, but no one remembers anyone fitting Tillett's description renting a car for such a short period and putting that much mileage on it."

"All of which proves nothing. If Tillett's our killer, he could have planted the poison in Edith and Sophia's vitamins and waited for them to take them. He didn't have to be in town when it happened. It's bad luck we weren't able to pinpoint the vitamins as the source of cyanide when Edith died. Maybe we could have saved Sophia."

Bill stretched and yawned. Fatigue made him look older than his age.

"Thanks for your help," I said.

"Some help. I turned up nada."

"Maybe. Time will tell." But I was running out of time.

Bill's head fell back against the top of the chair back, and he began to snore softly. Watching him, I felt a peculiar stinging behind my eyelids. It couldn't be tears. A cop can't be a slave to emotion, and I hadn't cried since my father died. The sensation was probably a side effect from my allergies. I propped Bill's feet on a hassock, covered him with an afghan and planted a kiss on his forehead before turning out the lights as I left.

Coffee, they say, doesn't sober you up. It just makes you wide-awake drunk. That's how I felt as I drove to the station after leaving Bill snoozing in my living room. Pelican Bay had a high percentage of retirees who hit the sheets early, so the post-midnight streets were quiet and deserted. As I crossed the trail, I glimpsed a dark silhouette on its path. Many flouted the sundown closing regulations, so the shadow could have been a cat burglar or an insomniac walking his dog.

When I entered the CID office, Adler sat hunched over his desk, pecking at his sticky keyboard. With the current department budget crunch, new computers had been scratched from this year's budget. Adler's sandy hair stood in peaks, as if he'd spent the evening running his fingers through it and coaxing it on end.

"You still here?" I asked.

"I was just leaving you some notes." He handed me the page the printer spit out.

"I have a few reports to type myself. Bill came in from Boca tonight. Tillett's alibi is a wash. We can't prove or disprove."

Adler's satisfied grin predicted good news. "I kept drawing blanks on Dorman's address, until I remembered Tillett said he's a bodybuilder. Tonight I called every health club and gym in the yellow pages until I hit the Body Shop on U.S. 19, north of the mall. Dorman works out there seven days a week."

"Was he there when you called?"

Adler shook his head. "It was late and the gym was closing, but the manager furnished an interesting piece of news. Dorman's new place of employment. He's working as a waiter until he lands another med-tech job."

The look on Adler's face reminded me of Jessica's when she'd opened her bunny book. "Are you going to tell me or do I have to take you into the back room and beat it out of you with a rubber hose?"

"Dorman's working at Sophia's."

"For Lester Morelli?"

"Yeah. Whaddaya make of that?" Adler ran his fingers through his hair, realigning the vertical tufts.

"Coincidence?"

"You don't believe in coincidences, remember?" He slipped his jacket off the back of his chair and pulled it on. "I'm going home for a few hours' sleep. You want me to question Dorman in the morning?"

"I'd planned to interview the staff at Sophia's tomorrow, so I'll catch Dorman then. How about running up to Tarpon Springs and checking out Anastasia Gianakis, Vasily's widow. There was bad blood between her husband and Sophia Morelli. I want to know how bad."

When Adler left, I sat at my desk and began pounding out accounts of my interviews with Tillett's patients and staff and Bill's findings in Boca Raton. By 3:00 a.m., both coffee and Benadryl had worn off. I wandered back to the processing room, located an empty holding cell and stretched out on the metal bunk. If I hadn't been too tired to scratch, my hives would have kept me awake.

Someone flicked on the overhead fluorescent light and awakened me. Darcy Wilkins stood in the doorway. "The chief wants to see you, on the double."

I glanced at my watch—6:45 a.m. "The chief never comes in before nine."

"He's here now, and he's not happy. If I were you, girl, I'd haul—"

"I'm coming."

I stumbled on stiff legs to the locker room, splashed cold water on my face, brushed my teeth so I wouldn't slay the chief with my first exhalation, and ran a comb through the hair flattened on one side of my head. Shelton had been in a royal snit when Edith Wainwright was murdered. Sophia Morelli's demise probably had him frothing at the mouth. I approached his office with trepidation.

The chief sat with his elbows propped on his desk and held his head in his hands. When he glanced up, he looked worse than I felt. His gray Brooks Brothers suit, red power tie and immaculate dress shirt couldn't counteract the devastation on his face.

"Sit down, Skerritt." He waved me into a chair across from his desk. "Coffee?"

The sight of Shelton playing gracious host unnerved me even more than his appearance. I accepted coffee in a china mug embossed with the PBPD logo and waited.

The chief settled back in his chair. "I suppose you're wondering why I'm here so early, dressed to the nines?"

"The Morelli murder?" I braced for the brunt of his legendary temper.

"Partly. But that's not the worst of it."

I nodded and sipped my coffee, still expecting an explosion.

"The city council met last night," he said in a toneless voice. "Councilman Ulrich presented a proposal, designed to ease the city budget crunch by several million dollars."

"That's good. It'll take the pressure off the department to cut back."

"Under Ulrich's proposal, there won't be a department. He wants the city to contract police protection through the county sheriff's office. I've called a press conference for ten o'clock to comment on the proposal."

Stunned, I simply looked at him. If the city disbanded the department, I could retire and walk away, but Darcy, Steve Johnson, Lenny Jacobs, Adler, who'd just bought a house, what would happen to them and the others if their jobs disappeared? "What's the beef? Doesn't Ulrich think we're doing our jobs?"

Shelton swiped a palm over his bald head, and the weariness in the movement suggested he'd had less sleep than I had. "It's strictly a bottom-line issue, nothing to do with the service, Ulrich insists."

"Ulrich is an idiot," I said. "It has to do with loyalty and people's lives. Why be incorporated as a city, if not to provide police and fire protection?"

Anger sent a surge of adrenaline through me, aggravating my already inflamed skin. I felt sorry for Shelton, who'd now have to walk a thin line between defending his department and placating the council.

"I've posted a memo," he said, "explaining what I can, but I need your help, Maggie."

"I'm no politician, Chief. This one's in your court."

"If you don't find this murderer soon, Ulrich will have more ammunition for his cause, an implication that since we can't do the job, we might as well turn everything over to the sheriff."

"Adler and I are working overtime as it is. Even with

Bill Malcolm assisting gratis, we can't conduct interviews and follow leads fast enough."

"I understand—" He stopped abruptly and peered over the desk at me. "What's the matter with your face?"

"Allergies," I snapped. "I'm allergic to murder."

He sighed and pinched the bridge of his nose wearily. "You have to do the best you can with what you have to work with. Between the double homicide and Ulrich's proposal, the department's under siege now, and you're the point man. Everyone's counting on you to make us look good."

"If you want results, I need more detectives, not more pressure." I searched for a remnant of the infamous Shelton temper in his haggard face, and the lack of it scared me.

He stood and shrugged, looking shriveled and impotent in his expensive suit. "Pressure's all I've got to offer. I have to write a statement for the press. Good luck, Maggie."

I walked back to my office, ignoring Darcy's inquisitive stare. For once, everything in my life, my work, my future, my relationship with my family, were all headed in the same direction.

Right down the toilet.

CHAPTER 11

A pod of dolphins broke the glassy surface of the bay and provided an impromptu show for diners on Sophia's palazzo. I finished a bran muffin and melon slice, shoved the dishes aside and drew a grid on my legal pad while I waited for the breakfast crowd to disperse.

Down the left margin, I listed everyone connected to Edith or Sophia. Across the top, I made columns for motivation and alibis. By the time I'd finished the page and polished off a carafe of coffee, I was alone on the terrace.

"Can I bring you anything else?" A matronly waitress, who moved as if her feet hurt, placed my check on the table.

"If the maître d' is in, I'd like to talk with him."

A few minutes later, a gray-haired man in a dark suit with a continental cut approached my table and introduced himself as Antonio Stavropoulos. "Is there a problem?"

I produced my badge. "I'm investigating the death of Sophia Morelli, and I have a few questions."

He sat opposite me and smoothed a wisp of snowy mustache. "I began working for George Gianakis when Sophia was a baby. When George died, I worked for her. She was like my own daughter. What can I do to help?"

"Tell me about her."

"Sophia was a beautiful child. Her papa had wanted a son, but when God did not smile on him, he doted on his daughter. Taught her everything about the hotel and restaurant business, and promised her that Sophia's, named, as she was, for her grandmother, would be hers someday."

"She liked running the restaurant?"

Antonio snapped his fingers at the waitress and pointed to the empty coffee carafe. When she scurried away, he turned back to me. "She loved working alongside her papa. When George died ten years ago, she was heartbroken."

"She was almost thirty then. Had she never married?"

"She couldn't bear the thought of leaving her papa. And even if she could, George thought no man good enough for his Sophia. Called them all fortune hunters. And why not? What man wouldn't wish to own such a place as this?" He threw open his arms, taking in the broad terrace, the waterfront view and the pink-stuccoed restaurant designed like a doge's palace. "George patterned it after Ringling's Cà d'Zan in Sarasota."

"And after George died?"

Antonio straightened his lapels and leaned forward. "Sophia tried to fill the hole that her papa's death left in her heart with *baklava* and *galatabouriko*. She grew heavier and heavier, and then the diabetes and heart problems began."

"How did she meet Lester Morelli?"

"Six years ago I hired him as a waiter. He was kind to Sophia, made her laugh. Before anyone knows what's going on—" he snapped his fingers in the air "—Sophia is marrying Lester and he is running the restaurant. As ill as she was, she was happy to have a man to lean on once again." Antonio's resentment was poorly concealed.

"Was that a problem?"

He shrugged. "Lester is a good manager, and Sophia's health would not allow her to continue but—"

He paused as the waitress brought a fresh carafe of coffee, clean cups and a platter of the Greek pastries that had ruined Sophia's health and figure. He poured coffee for us both and helped himself to a pastry after my virtuous refusal.

"You were saying about Lester's management," I prodded.

"The restaurant keeps its reputation, and business is good, but it is not the same."

"I don't understand."

"Lester Morelli is not Greek, not one of us. He will always be an outsider."

Now that Lester owned the restaurant, with that attitude, Antonio might find himself the outsider. "Did you know Vasily Gianakis?"

He swallowed a bite of *baklava* and dabbed his mustache with his napkin. "When brother turns against brother is always sad."

"Why did they quarrel?"

"Vasily stole his brother's sweetheart."

"Anastasia?"

"Both brothers wanted her, but Anastasia had eyes only for Vasily. He was younger, more handsome. But also poorer."

My mother had told me about the brothers' falling out, but I'd forgotten most of it. "Didn't their father leave them both an equal share of the restaurant, resort and real estate holdings?"

"Yes, but that is the saddest part. George was frugal, always pinching his pennies, but Vasily—" he shook his head. "Vasily was a big spender, bought a large home, fancy cars, a yacht, all for his beloved Anastasia. Within a year after receiving his inheritance, it was gone."

"How could he run through a fortune so quickly?"

"There was very little cash. Most of the brothers' money was tied up jointly in real estate, the restaurant and the resort. Vasily couldn't liquidate his holdings without George's consent. George refused.

"So Vasily lost everything?"

"No, George paid off his brother's debts, but he took title to Vasily's half of everything as collateral. Vasily was never able to pay off the debts and interest, so George called in his note. The brothers never spoke to each other again. And Vasily never forgave Sophia for inheriting what he considered rightfully his.

"And Anastasia?"

"While Vasily was alive, she obeyed his wishes and shunned Sophia. But after her husband's death, she made peace with her niece."

"Peace?"

"She would come to the restaurant and have lunch with Sophia and invite Sophia to her house. But Sophia only, never Lester."

"Seems odd she'd bury the hatchet so quickly after

so many years of animosity." I traced Anastasia's name in the left column of my chart.

"Sophia claimed both of them were glad to see an end to the brothers' hatefulness, but Lester thought otherwise. Who knows, maybe this time, Lester is right."

"About what?"

"I usually leave the gossiping to the old women," he said, "but I want Sophia's killer caught. And if Anastasia Gianakis had anything to do with that sweet girl's death, I hope she burns in hell."

"What makes you think Anastasia's involved?"

"Lester told Sophia her aunt was only trying to ingratiate herself to persuade Sophia to include Anastasia in her will."

I needed a scorecard to keep the players straight in this game of family intrigue. "Wouldn't that be the other way around? Anastasia's much older than Sophia was. Why would the older woman want to be included in her niece's will?"

"Because the reason Sophia started attending the weight-loss clinic three years ago was that her doctors expected her to die any minute."

"Did she add Anastasia to her will?"

"No one ever told me, but Sophia was crazy about her husband. I'm sure she left him everything."

"Then why would Anastasia wish to harm Sophia?"

"For the dish that is best served cold." He speared the last bite of *baklava* and popped it into his mouth.

"Revenge? But Sophia did nothing to Anastasia."

"Family hatreds are seldom logical, Detective."

Neither was murder. I could find no trace of reason in either Edith's or Sophia's death. "Does Lester have enemies, anyone who might try to hurt him through his wife?"

Antonio ran a finger inside his crisp collar as if it was suddenly too tight. "I have already told you there are those of us who resent him because he is an outsider, but none of us would hurt Sophia. That would be like cutting off a nose to hurt one's face."

"Anyone else? Dissatisfied customers? Canceled suppliers?"

"If there were unhappy customers, I would know. As for the wholesalers, I am unaware of any problem, but that does not mean it does not exist."

"Were Lester and Sophia happy together?"

His mouth twisted in an ironic smile. "Who is to say what is happiness between a man and wife? Did they fight and throw things in the presence of others? Not here. Since she started her strict diet, Sophia avoided the restaurant like a reformed alcoholic shuns a cantina, so I've seen little of her the past two years. But when she was here, I witnessed no friction between them."

"Lester Morelli will inherit a fortune. Does he strike you as the type who would murder for money?"

"Why should he? He had it all, anyway." Antonio's narrow lips curved in a frown. "When he came in last night, he looked terrible. He's taking it very hard."

"He came to work the day after his wife died?"

"He was here. I did not say he worked. He shut himself in his office with a bottle of Jack Daniel's. By the time we closed at midnight, the bottle was empty and Lester was falling-down drunk. Brent drove him home."

"Brent Dorman?"

Antonio lifted his eyebrows. "You know him?"

"I'd like to question him. What time does he come in?"

Antonio shot out his wrist and checked a steel-and-gold Rolex. "He should be here now. Would you like me to send him to you?" He stood and adjusted his jacket.

"I won't keep him long. But first, was Lester here Friday evening between five and seven o'clock?"

"He was here all day Friday, from morning till midnight."

"And you're certain he didn't leave between the hours I mentioned?"

"Every Friday from five until midnight, Lester works on the books, brings them up to date for the week. He was in his office last Friday as usual."

"And Dorman, did he work Friday?"

Antonio's eyes widened. "Only until four o'clock. He had pulled a muscle in his back, so I sent him home. He returned to work on Saturday."

"Fully recovered?"

"He appeared to be. Why don't you ask him?" He bowed with continental grace and left.

I scribbled a few notes from my interview with Antonio, then walked down the stairs toward the landing that served as a dock for the restaurant. Boaters often tied up there long enough for a meal at the palazzo, but this morning the slips were empty and the bay deserted. The setting mocked me with its serenity. Somewhere in this tranquil community was a killer who had murdered twice and could strike again at any minute.

"Detective Skerritt?"

I jumped, almost dropping my notepad into the water. A stocky man, built like a steel fireplug, had approached without a sound. "Brent Dorman?"

"Yeah. What can I do for you?"

"You used to work for Dr. Tillett?"

"This is about the fatso murders, isn't it." His grin did little to soften the hard lines of his young face. "Bet there's a bunch of hefties out there now, pushing away those extra helpings at the thought of someone just waiting to whack 'em."

I sat on the balustrade that edged the lower terrace. Dorman perched beside me with his massive arms crossed over his chest.

"You don't care much for heavy people, do you?" I said.

He grimaced like a man with a bad taste in his mouth. "If they don't respect themselves enough to keep fit, why should I respect them?"

"Is that what you told Dr. Tillett when he fired you?"

"Hey, fat people disgust me. Lots of people disgust me, but that doesn't mean I'd kill them." He clenched his arms tighter across his chest, and his powerful biceps strained against the fabric of his white dress shirt.

"Antonio tells me you left work early Friday."

"We had a big luncheon party, a bunch of blue-haired old biddies raising money for some charity. When I was clearing up afterward, I stacked a tray too heavy, picked it up wrong and pulled a muscle in my back. If I'd kept working, it would have tightened up, and I'd have been out for a week."

"You went home?"

"I went to the Body Shop for a massage, then I went home."

"What time was that?"

"I left here before four. Jake worked me right in, and I was home by five, five-fifteen."

"You live alone?"

"I got a garage apartment over on Tangerine Street. Ain't much, but I couldn't afford my other place after Tillett let me go."

"Did you see or talk to anyone when you arrived home?"

"What is this? I told you I didn't whack Moby Edith or Ms. Morelli, either. Her husband's a good guy, gave me this job when I needed it bad. Why should I hurt her?" Sweat beaded on his forehead.

"Is there anyone who saw you at home Friday night?"

"No. I took a muscle relaxant and slept till time to get ready for work Saturday."

"And you worked all day and never left the restaurant?" I was groping in the dark, hoping to bump into something, anything, significant.

"Yeah, that's right—aw, shit." His confident manner evaporated and his muscles seemed to lose their tone. "I did leave the restaurant once. I made a delivery in the van."

"Where?"

"To the Morelli place on Pelican Point. Every few days, Mr. Morelli has me restock his refrigerator. Saves his wife from having to shop and cook while she's on that liquid diet."

"Did you see Sophia?"

"No." He perspired in the cool sea air. "Mr. Morelli always gives me a key so I don't have to disturb her. But all I did was unlock the door, put the containers in the refrigerator and leave."

I took down his new address and told him I'd be in touch. Brent Dorman was an obnoxious bigot, but I'd need a better motive than prejudice to book him for murder.

I interviewed several other waiters and Lester's chef, but no one could shed any light on Sophia's death. The woman had been loved and respected by the help, and while most expressed resentment of Lester as an outsider, all confirmed his devotion to his wife.

The early luncheon crowd was gathering as I passed through the main room with its ceiling that opened to the second floor. Marble columns supported an encircling gallery with doorways leading to private dining rooms. Linen-draped tables, tucked beneath the balcony in secluded alcoves with tall windows, sported Reserved cards. The room's elegance, more ostentatious than the yacht club, failed to intimidate me. Unlike the exclusivity of my mother's favorite haunt, the ambience of Sophia's could be enjoyed by anyone with a few extra dollars or a major credit card.

I walked toward my car and squinted in the noonday sun. A sleek Mercedes glided past me and parked in a reserved space at the side of the building. Lester Morelli climbed out slowly, as if his muscles ached. Mirrored aviator glasses hid his eyes, so I couldn't read his expression or tell if he recognized me. He entered the restaurant by a side door marked Private.

Although the sun hadn't passed the yardarm, I expected Antonio had Lester's bottle of Jack Daniel's ready and waiting.

CHAPTER 12

Adler stood by the window in the CID office when I returned to the station.

"Don't sit down," he said. "I'm taking you to lunch."

"I spent all morning in a restaurant. I'll just grab something from the vending machine."

"No restaurants." He gripped my elbow and maneuvered me out of the office and down the hall. "We can use some fresh air to clear our heads."

I climbed into his new Toyota SUV, and the aroma of garlic and onions hit me. "What have you got in here, a deli?"

"Stopped for takeout before I left Tarpon Springs."

His too-hearty attitude didn't fool me. By now the whole station knew about Ulrich's proposal to disband the department. Dave had a new house, new car and new baby to pay for. His cheerfulness probably covered panic.

We drove east along Pelican Creek to Pioneer Park,

a natural hammock of live oaks crisscrossed with nature trails. Dave parked in the empty lot, and we walked
to a shaded picnic table beside the creek. Above the
tannin-dyed waters, an anhinga roosted in a wax myr-
tle and spread its wings to dry.

Dave carried two paper sacks, one grease-stained, the
other threatening to break at the bottom from mois-
ture. He swiped a few strands of Spanish moss off the
table and unpacked the bags.

"Gyros." He handed me a sandwich the size of a
football. "Greek salads and cold drinks."

I popped the top on a sweating can and lifted it in
salute. "The dieter's downfall. I can consume a thousand calories in one sitting, but if I wash it down with
Diet Coke, somehow I feel virtuous."

His boyish face split into a grin. "Want me to run
down to Dr. Tillett's and have them whip you up a diet
shake?"

"I want to be thin, not dead." I shuddered at the
thought. "Which reminds me, what did you find out
about Anastasia?"

"She is one strange woman. Like something out of
an Alfred Hitchcock movie."

"Antonio, the maître d' at Sophia's, said she was so
beautiful years ago, the Gianakis brothers fought over

her." I lifted anchovies and feta cheese off the mound of lettuce in a round container, set them aside and dug beneath the greens and sliced beets for potato salad.

"She's sixty-five, shaped like a washing machine, smokes like a chimney and dresses entirely in black. She lives in a tiny house a block from the sponge docks, and I stopped counting housecats when I hit twelve."

"Feeble?"

"As in too feeble to get around? No way. She has her own car, tends her own garden, even works several hours a week in a gift shop she owns on Dodecanese Boulevard."

"Was she upset by Sophia's murder?"

"She's madder than a wet hen. Blames Lester Morelli."

I paused with the gyro halfway to my mouth. "That's a twist. Everyone I've talked to sings his praises as the model husband. What's her beef?"

"Claims he wants the Gianakis fortune all for himself and would do anything to get it. She says Sophia was flying to Athens to get away from him—and to break the news to her relatives that she was filing for divorce."

"Was Anastasia credible?"

He took a large bite of his sandwich and chewed thoughtfully. "Not completely. She couldn't give me the name of anyone else who could corroborate her charge. Says Sophia told her everything in confidence. She acts a little crazy, but she definitely has her own agenda."

"She still after Vasily's half of the Gianakis fortune?"

"Not half. All of it. According to her, Sophia left everything to Lester, but had Lester died first, Anastasia would be the secondary beneficiary."

I tried to picture Lester as the killer, but it clashed with everything more than a dozen witnesses had said about him and his relationship with his wife. "So if Lester was convicted of Sophia's murder, Anastasia would be a multimillionaire."

"Like I said, she's one spooky character. But capable of murder?" He shrugged.

The more I uncovered, the more tangled this case became. "When did Anastasia see Sophia last?"

Adler scooped up the cheese and anchovies I'd set aside and plopped them on his salad. "That's the interesting part. She visited Sophia Friday afternoon to say goodbye before her trip to Athens."

"And between five and seven when Edith died?"

"Anastasia says she left Sophia's a little after five and drove straight home to feed her cats. But none of her neighbors saw her. I checked."

I played out a scenario in my head. Anastasia leaves poison in her niece's vitamin bottle, drives to Edith Wainwright's and somehow poisons her, maybe with cyanide-laced chocolates, then pins the blame on Lester, who, if convicted, forfeits his inheritance to Anastasia. But why not poison only Sophia and then blame Lester? "Did Anastasia know Edith?"

He shook his head. "Only what she'd read in the paper about her murder."

I shoved my unfinished salad and sandwich aside, pulled out the notes I'd taken that morning and filled Adler in, not only on what Antonio and Dorman had told me, but my impressions as well.

"What do you think?" I asked when I'd finished.

"Beats the hell out of me. If both women hadn't been killed with the same poison, I'd say their connection through the clinic is only a weird coincidence."

"Mick's report is in. The lab hasn't turned up any contaminants in the other vitamins or diet drinks, and the FDA has no reports of similar cases involving these products. We can't completely rule out product-tampering yet, but my instincts tell me the killer's right here and knew both these women."

"It would help if your instincts could be more specific." Adler swigged his Classic Coke and wiped his mouth with the back of his hand. "Doc Cline's toxicology report confirms both women were killed by potassium ferricyanide."

"Did she detail the commercial uses for the compound?"

"Yeah. Doc's thorough."

"We'll put together a list of local suppliers when we get back to the station, then check them out, see if any of them know any of our suspects." I resisted the impulse to cross my arms on the table, lay my head down and sleep. Just the thought of interviewing dozens of suppliers in the Tampa Bay area who might have sold poison to the killer made me even more tired.

Adler finished his sandwich and pointed to mine. "You gonna eat that?"

My appetite had disappeared, and, in addition to suffering from fatigue, my arms and back itched. "No, go ahead."

He reached for my gyro. "How many murders have you worked?"

"Too many."

I closed my eyes to the memory of small, white bodies, bloated with saltwater. Bill and I had never tracked down the killer who terrorized Tampa years ago, kidnapping and murdering children before dumping their bodies in the bay. The murders had ceased as abruptly as they'd begun, leading us to believe the perp had either died or moved to another part of the country after we'd turned up the heat. My skin erupted in new blotches at the recollection.

Adler gobbled the sandwich, gathered up the empty containers and papers, stuffed them in a nearby trash receptacle and sat at the table again. He rolled his drink can between his wide palms, staring at it as if searching for answers. He hadn't brought me here to talk about the case. He could have done that in the office.

"You heard the chief's announcement," he said.

"He told me about it this morning. He hopes we can solve these murders in a hurry to make the department look good."

He clenched his hands, crushing the aluminum can. "We both know that's not going to happen. We're going around in circles, getting nowhere."

"All we need is a break. That one small piece that makes the whole picture fall into place." My pep talk was as much for me as my partner. I'd been consumed by doubts.

"I won't do anything," he said, "until I've talked with Sharon, but my mind's made up. I can't wait for the city council to decide. I'm submitting applications to the Clearwater and St. Pete departments."

His eyes filled with pain, and I wanted to assure him that everything would work out, but local politics and politicians were never predictable. In Adler's place, I'd be doing the same thing.

"If the sheriff takes over city protection," I said, "he'll have to hire extra deputies—"

"I have to think of my family. I can't take a chance on waiting." He smashed the crumpled can against the table. "How do they expect us to concentrate on our work when our jobs are hanging—"

"We have to." I held up my hands against his protests. "I know, that's easy for me to say. I can collect my pension and walk away. But if we nail the bastard who's been supplementing diets with cyanide, maybe we can help the others in the department keep their jobs."

He tossed the can into the trash, stood and brushed away a few leaves that clung to his jeans. "You remind me of my mom, always looking on the bright side."

"Thanks, Adler. You just made my day." Feeling older than my years, I followed him to his car.

With the exception of a few recent upscale developments, the farther inland a house from the waters of

Pelican Bay, the lower the real estate values. Peter Castleberry lived on the eastern edge of the city in a house with peeling paint that might once have sheltered migrant grove workers.

A broken concrete walk led across the sandy yard to the front porch, where aged screening, pulled away from its splicing, draped over scraggly plumbago bushes flanking the front stoop. Stacks of yellowed newspapers and magazines covered the porch floor, except for a clear swath to the front door. I rang the bell, and it buzzed in an interior room like an angry metallic insect.

The floor trembled beneath my feet as Castleberry approached. He jerked the door open and scowled. "Whaddaya want?"

"I have a few more questions. They won't take long."

He grimaced and stepped aside for me to enter. A white Persian cat shot across the room and down a hallway.

"I already told you everything I know," he whined.

My questions were forgotten as I surveyed his living room. Unlike the clutter on his porch, the room, bare of all furniture except a television and an oversize recliner, had the sparse, sleek appearance of an art gallery. Track lighting along the ceiling illuminated a series of poster-size, framed photographs.

"These are gorgeous." I moved closer to one wall to examine the black-and-white scenes: clusters of masts at the marina, the dunes of Pelican Beach, a sailboat with its spinnaker puffed with wind on the bay, a night-blooming cirrus strangling a bleached dead tree trunk. The masterful shading of black and white seemed more vibrant than the gaudy tones of Kodachrome. "Did you take these?"

His prickly demeanor softened at my praise. "I told you I was a photographer."

"You ought to contact the art centers, arrange a show." I wasn't feeding his ego. His pictures reminded me of Clyde Butcher's shots of the Everglades and Panhandle beaches.

"That's what Les told me."

"Lester Morelli?"

"Several months back we had like a show-and-tell at our clinic meeting. Les saw my photograph of Pelican Beach when he dropped Sophia off. Asked me if I'd consider selling it."

I remembered the beachscape above the fireplace in the Morelli living room. "I've seen it."

"It was one of my favorites. Les came by and looked at all of them, but he liked that one best. Bought it for Sophia as a surprise."

Without his belligerent posture, Castleberry was almost friendly. He dragged a straight chair in from the adjoining dining room and offered it to me before dropping his bulk into his recliner.

"Did me a real favor, Les did. I needed the money. Disability checks don't go very far."

"So you know Morelli well?"

"Not well. Just enough to speak to. But he's a great guy, and he paid generously for the picture."

I jumped as something rubbed against my ankle. The Persian had returned to slink around the legs of my chair and purr like a distant motor.

"Come here, baby. Come to Daddy," Castleberry crooned in his reedy voice. The cat leaped into his lap and lifted its head to have its throat scratched. "This is Fluffy. She's good company."

"Edith Wainwright had a cat, a Siamese."

"I know. She got her the same place I got Fluffy. From Sophia's aunt."

"Anastasia Gianakis?" The woman had told Adler she didn't know Edith.

"At one of our meetings, Edith and I talked about how lonely living by ourselves is, and Karen suggested we get a pet. We both said we liked cats, and Sophia mentioned that her aunt took in strays until she found homes for them. A few days later, Anastasia showed up on my doorstep with a cat carrier and Fluffy. Now she's like one of the family."

"Anastasia?"

He looked blank for an instant, then shook his head. "Fluffy. She's like my own kid."

"Did Anastasia take a cat to Edith, too?"

"Yeah, same day. She had the Siamese in the car with her. She was waiting until after five when Edith got home from work, so she came in, had a glass of tea and looked at my exhibit. She left the Siamese in its carrier on the porch, and the damn thing cried like a baby the whole time." He shifted his weight in his big chair and looked over my shoulder, avoiding my eyes. "What happened to her?"

"Edith?"

"The cat."

"Animal control took it."

His fingers tightened on Fluffy's fur. "What'll they do with her?"

"Put her up for adoption, but if no one claims her…" Strange how he showed more empathy for the cat than the young woman whose life had ended so violently.

"Can I get you something?" he asked. "Iced tea? A soda?"

"I'd like to see the rest of your pictures, if you don't mind."

"Mind? I'm flattered. Take your time." He hoisted himself to his feet and shadowed me as I examined the rest of his works. He talked of f-stops, light meters, filters and lenses, and I let him ramble until he mentioned his darkroom.

"Do you develop your own film?"

"That's half the challenge, the only way to get the results I'm striving for. Want to see how it's done?"

I followed him to a cramped, windowless room at the back of the house with a counter, sink, rows of developing trays and drying lines stretched from wall to wall. He launched into a detailed account of the developing process.

Twenty minutes later when I pulled away, Castleberry, wearing a congenial smile, waved to me from the sagging porch.

I waved in return, but my smile was not for Castleberry. I was thinking of the brown, crystal-filled jar with a gold-and-red Kodak logo tucked among the chemicals and developing fluids on the darkroom shelf. The label read Potassium Ferricyanide.

CHAPTER 13

Morning sunlight glinted off a life-size angel of white marble, hovering on its granite pedestal above the crowd of mourners in Pilgrims Rest, Pelican Bay's oldest cemetery. Streaks, etched on the statue's cheeks by a century of rain and bird droppings, created the illusion of tears.

The melodic chant of the Greek Orthodox priest carried on the breeze to the hillock where Adler and I stood in the shade of a cypress tree to observe the funeral of Sophia Morelli.

Edith Wainwright's body had been flown to Michigan for burial beside her parents, and according to the local funeral home, no one had appeared to pay their final respects.

Lester Morelli, flanked by black-clad mourners, sat erect and unmoving before his wife's flower-covered coffin. His gaze locked on the blanket of sweetheart roses, but even at a distance, I could see his red-rimmed eyes and the wetness of tears on his face.

"I've never laid eyes on most of these people," Adler whispered.

I leaned toward him and whispered back, "Some are Sophia's relatives from Greece. I met them at the wake last night at the Morelli house."

"And Morelli's family?"

"He says he's an orphan, that Sophia was the only family he had." Morelli had been a gracious host the previous night, but strain and emotion had hardened the contours of his face and made him appear older. I'd detected a touch of frost in the air between him and Sophia's relatives, but Greek families are a clannish lot, slow to accept outsiders, as Antonio had told me.

At the final *amen*, the crowd dispersed. Karen Englewood, Richard Tillett and Marilee Ginsberg went directly to their cars. Ted and Janet Trask walked away with two other couples I recognized as Morelli neighbors. Antonio and others from the restaurant shook hands solemnly with Lester before leaving. Sophia's black-clad relatives climbed into stretch limousines, all except one, a short, stout woman who approached Lester after the others had left.

"That's her," Adler said. "Anastasia."

The woman pointed a black-gloved finger and poked Lester in the chest. She kept her voice low, but the anger in it carried her words to us.

"This is all your doing. Sophia Gianakis would be alive today if she hadn't married you!"

She continued to punch him with her finger, until Morelli batted her hand away. His features twisted, but whether from anger or grief was hard to tell. He leaned down inches from her face and spoke so softly we couldn't hear. She recoiled, sputtered as if at a loss for words and shook a clenched fist at him until a funeral home attendant intervened to lead Morelli to the remaining limo.

Anastasia stood alone beside Sophia's casket. The old woman caressed the polished wood surface, then slipped a rose from the casket spray and pressed it between the pages of her prayer book. She turned and stumbled over the uneven grass to her car, the last, besides mine, in the cemetery. When she passed us on her way out, her mouth was set in a thin, tight line.

"She's angry at Morelli," I said. "That's clear enough."

"Yeah, but because she thinks he killed Sophia, or is she just pissed because he gets the fortune that could have been hers?"

I glanced over the list of mourners I'd jotted in my notebook. "Brent Dorman didn't show."

"Why should he? He hated all Tillett's patients."

"But Morelli's his current boss, and the restaurant was closed for lunch today because of the funeral."

Adler grinned. "Just because the guy's a jerk doesn't mean he's a hypocrite."

"Any other brilliant conclusions?"

"I questioned him at his apartment early this morning," Adler said. "Caught him before he left for his daily workout. The guy's a survivalist, among other things. Every corner was stacked with rations, camping equipment and bottled water. Posters of bodybuilders and Schwarzenegger and Stallone armed to the teeth covered the walls. I didn't see any weapons, but I'll bet he has a cache somewhere. The place was littered with issues of *Soldier of Fortune*, *Gung Ho*, and *Guns & Ammo*."

"Dorman's an angry young man," I said, "but angry enough to kill?"

Adler scratched behind his ear, mussing his thick hair. In addition to his all-American good looks, he had a formidable mind. I could almost see the synapses firing behind his smiling eyes.

"Some of these guys," he said, "the real fanatics, might kill to prove their manhood. After talking with him and seeing how he lives, I'd bet if Dorman wanted to whack someone, he'd do it with his bare hands or a weapon. Not poison."

I conceded his point. "Where does that leave us?"

"Castleberry had the method, the bottle of potassium ferricyanide crystals. From the way you describe him, he seems mad at the world, ready to take his frustration out on anybody, but especially people like Sophia and Edith, who got in the way of the attention he craved from Tillett and Karen Englewood."

While we talked, two workers had removed the fake grass carpet that surrounded the gravesite, lowered Sophia's coffin into the sandy soil and begun filling the grave. The sound of earth hitting the casket depressed me. I thought of all the joys of living Sophia and Edith would never experience again, thanks to some crazy who'd decided to play God.

"I can't dispute the poison," I said, "but if you'd seen the photographs Castleberry created, you might think differently."

"Because the guy's an artist?" Adler shook his head. "Remember John Gacy? He was an artist. Painted clowns."

"The serial killer?"

"I rest my case. Some guy bought all Gacy's paintings after he was executed and destroyed them. Maybe someone will do the same for Castleberry."

I climbed into my car, removed a container of Benadryl gel from the glove compartment and smoothed it over my cheeks, forearms and the backs of my hands.

Adler got in beside me and fastened his shoulder harness. "This case really bugs you, doesn't it?"

"Nobody has the right to snuff out innocent people. But the worst thing is the feeling deep in my gut that the killer is only getting warmed up. If we don't stop him soon, we're going to have another victim on our hands."

"Him? You think it's a man?"

"I grew up in a time of gender inequality, Adler, when *he* was used as a general pronoun for male or female. I haven't ruled out anyone yet, and certainly not the women in our pool of suspects."

I started the car, drove toward the cemetery exit and caught one last glimpse of Sophia's grave in the rearview mirror. The gaping hole had been filled, smoothed over with dirt where the workers were laying fresh sod. In a matter of minutes, her presence had been erased forever from the face of the earth.

* * *

"You're back?" Mrs. Phillips glared at me over her bifocals.

"I told Archer I'd be here Friday for the information. He's expecting me." I didn't wait to be announced— walked straight past her into his office and closed the door on her astonished expression.

Archer looked up from the reams of printouts on his desk, then sprang to his feet. "Margaret, good to see you."

"Cut the fake cordiality, Archer. What have you got for me?"

"You picked yourself a couple of interesting boys. Who do you want first?" He removed two thick file folders from a basket on the corner of the desk.

"Morelli." I sank into the chair in front of him. "Can I have those files or should I take notes?"

"They're all yours, to cancel my debt, remember?" He pushed away from his desk, crossed the room with a bouncing step and yanked open the door. "Mama, run down to the grill and pick us up some sandwiches, will you?"

He watched her gather her purse and sweater, and waited until the latch had clicked behind her before he returned to his desk and Morelli's file. "This guy's parents divorced when he was four. His mother dumped him in a Catholic children's home in Illinois and disappeared. He was raised in a series of foster homes, with some claims of abuse, until eighteen. He served a brief and unremarkable hitch in the army, then moved to Los Angeles, where he lived until coming to Pelican Bay six years ago."

Morelli had been deserted by his parents, and now he'd lost his wife. I quelled a rush of sympathy. "Anything interesting in L.A.?"

"Worked as a waiter, did some modeling jobs and even a few gigs as a movie extra."

"Did you find out why he left?"

Archer ran a pudgy finger down the page. "Evicted from his apartment for overdue rent. Left behind a stack of bills that were eventually paid off."

"What's he worth now?"

He extracted another page from the sheaf in the folder. "Millions. Everything held in joint accounts with his wife."

"Did you find out why he came to Pelican Bay?"

"Nothing concrete in the file, but I can guess. In a tourist spot, he figured he'd find work as a waiter, and Florida has become a moviemaker's mecca. Maybe the guy had aspirations of stardom."

With no obvious success. But failure as an actor didn't make him a murderer. "What about Tillett?"

"This guy's in trouble, big time." Archer picked up a page and a trail of tractor paper four sheets long unfolded before him. "He's maxed out ten major credit cards, has second mortgages on both his house and clinic, and loans on both his cars. For the past year, he's knocked down only interest on all of those, and that's been paid late more often than not."

I nodded. "Tillett plays the dogs."

Archer let out a whistle. "Then he could also be out big money to loan sharks who don't keep the kind of records I can access. If that's the case, he's in deep doo-doo. The credit cards and mortgages alone are enough to make him desperate."

"Anything else suspicious?"

He shoved the files across the desk. "That's for you to decide. You're the dick, if you'll pardon the expression."

My tactics had made him angry, and I didn't blame him, but they'd also saved me weeks of digging. "Thanks, Archie. You've been a big help."

"Didn't have a choice, did I?" His grimacing smile propelled me toward the door.

I met his mother in the hall.

"Aren't you staying for lunch, Margaret? I bought tuna fish."

"I have to get back to work." I hurried toward the elevator.

"Take time to see a beauty consultant," she yelled after me. "Your makeup's still not right."

The Dock of the Bay, a rustic little restaurant on the opposite side of the marina from Sophia's, had been known in earlier days as a juke joint. The ancient Wurlitzer belted out a Willie Nelson ballad as I searched through the dim light for Bill Malcolm. The supper crowd had thinned and the serious drinking crowd hadn't arrived yet. I spotted Bill across the room, nursing a beer in a booth beside a window that framed a picture-postcard view of the marina basin.

I slumped onto the wooden bench across from him. "Sorry I'm late."

"You're working too hard." He called a waiter over and ordered burgers and fries for both of us, then reached across the table and took my hand. "When's the last time you read a book?"

I squeezed his rough fingers. "Give me a break. You know I'm lucky to skim the headlines in the *Times* every day."

"Reading's your favorite pastime, but if you've enjoyed a good novel since our trip to the Bahamas, I'll eat this place mat."

"I have Clancy's latest on my nightstand. Does that count?"

"Be serious, Margaret. You're not getting any younger. This pace has to wear on you. Every day, often for twenty-four hours at a time, you have to talk like a cop, think like a criminal and act like a hero. No wonder you break out in hives."

"I can't quit. Not now. It's been a week tonight since Edith Wainwright was killed, less since Sophia's murder, and I don't have a prime suspect. And I'd be getting even less sleep if it weren't for you. Any luck on the cyanide?"

Bill had spent the last three days interviewing suppliers who carried potassium ferricyanide.

"I've exhausted every source in the area, even checked as far as Tampa and Sarasota, and the mail-order suppliers. Nada on everyone, except Peter Castleberry. He's a regular at the photography store in Clearwater, buys all his supplies there, including potassium ferricyanide. It's used in Farmer's reducer formula for overdeveloped or overexposed negatives."

"You sound like an expert." The waiter set a mug of

cold beer in front of me. I took a sip and licked foam off my upper lip.

Bill pushed back his hair and exposed a creased, tanned forehead. "Where *isn't* that poison used? I've learned more about blueprint paper, wood stains, electroplating, etching and photography in the past three days than I ever wanted to know. But what good is it? You're right back where you started with Castleberry."

"Maybe." I told him what Archer Phillips had dug up for me. "Tillett's in big financial trouble. Sophia's million-dollar bequest gives him a powerful motive."

"And Morelli? He stands to gain more than Tillett."

"But Morelli already has access to all the money," I said, "and except for the crazy aunt in Tarpon Springs, everyone insists he was devoted to his wife."

"Maybe the devoted husband had a little action going on the side?" Bill spread ketchup over his basket of French fries.

"When? He works eighteen-hour days and spends all his time off at home." I picked up the thick sandwich, a real hamburger, not the paste-and-cardboard fast-food kind. I'd had only a cup of yogurt for lunch, and my stomach grumbled with hunger. "Adler thinks Castleberry's our man—"

The beeper on my belt sounded.

"When are you going to give in and buy a cell phone?" Bill asked.

"When I'm ready to have my privacy invaded 24/7 by anyone with a phone." I put down my burger and scooted off the bench. "There's a pay phone in the lobby."

Bill grabbed my hand. "You have to eat. You can call when you're finished."

"But I'd worry. It's probably something that can wait. I'll call and find out."

I should have taken his advice. I returned to the table after taking the message from the station, cast a longing look at my full plate and picked up my purse. "No supper tonight."

"What's up?"

"Must be something in the water. Another homicide."

"Have they identified the victim?"

"Adult male is all they gave me. Killed on the trail."

Bill asked the waiter to put our order in a bag and add a couple of large black coffees. He rose to his feet. "I'm coming with you."

CHAPTER 14

I drove south on Edgewater, turned onto Windward Lane and passed Karen Englewood's house. Two blocks east, where Windward intersected the trail, a knot of emergency vehicles with pulsing red-and-blue lights marked the scene. Above them, a sheriff's chopper hovered and swept the trail and adjacent yards with its searchlights.

In front of the yellow tape that blocked entrance to the trail from Windward, three preteen boys gawked at officers whose flashlights winked in the darkness a hundred feet down the path.

"It's after ten," I said to the boys. "Shouldn't you go home?"

"Cops told us to hang around," the largest boy said. "We found the body."

I turned my flashlight toward him and recognized the close-cropped sandy hair and pugnacious face wall-papered with freckles. "Jason?"

"Yeah, it's me."

Jason McLeod had a rap sheet as long as my arm for vandalism, B and Es and car theft, but as a juvenile had spent almost no time in detention. The court consistently released him to the custody of his alcoholic mother, who earned her booze money through prostitution.

"Tell me what happened," I said. I sensed Bill's quiet presence behind me. He'd do anything I asked, but until I asked, he'd stay in the background. He knew the protocol. This was my investigation.

Jason wiped his nose with the cuff of a grimy sweatshirt. "We were racing on the trail. We can't see, but that's what makes it fun, zooming through the dark, like outer space. Then my bike hit something and sent me flying."

"You struck the body?" I asked.

"Naw, the dead guy's bike. But when I fell, I rolled right up against him. That's when we cut out of there to the nearest yard and asked the lady to call the cops."

"Did you see anyone else on the trail?"

"Just somebody running."

"A man or a woman?"

Jason hunched his skinny shoulders. "Too dark. Couldn't tell."

"Which way did the runner go?"

"Headed this way, south, just before we found the body. After that, I didn't pay no attention."

"You boys better get home. And stay off the trail after dark or the next body found could be yours."

Jason thrust his chin out and his two scruffy cohorts followed suit.

"I ain't afraid," Jason said with a snarl.

And he wasn't, of either the law or the terrors of the night. Jason would probably end up in Raiford or the morgue, or both. I doubted even boot camp could turn him around. One of the frustrations of my job was watching a kid like Jason slide deeper into a life of crime and me without any way to put on the brakes.

Bill loaded their bikes into the trunk of my Volvo and herded the boys into the car to drive them home, while I trekked down the blacktop toward the crime scene. The wide recreational path, a straight shot through the darkness, broken at block-long intervals by intersecting streets, was eerily quiet. I trained my flashlight over broad grassy swaths dotted with lantana verbena and gaillardia that lined the asphalt and scanned thick hedges of Turk's cap, viburnum and ligustrum that homeowners had planted to screen their properties from the trail's users.

Midway down the block, an adult tricycle lay on its side in the middle of the trail, its left wheel in the air and its rider sprawled alongside, his legs tangled in the pedals.

The helicopter passed overhead, and its searchlights illuminated the scene in unnatural light. The victim lay on his side with his face pressed into a pool of blood on the asphalt. Behind his left ear, a small dark circle marked the entrance wound. I wasn't looking forward to seeing what the bullet had done when it exited on the other side of his face.

Adler came up behind me. "We gotta quit meeting like this, Maggie."

"Call the crime-scene unit," I said, "and ask the fire department to bring floodlights and a generator. And keep everyone else out of here."

"Another clinic member?"

"Peter Castleberry. Our list at the clinic is now down to four."

Dawn filtered through the Australian pines that lined the eastern edge of the trail. With daylight, I could begin a more thorough investigation of the scene. During the night, Adler and I had already interviewed the homeowners whose properties backed up to the murder site, but no one had seen or heard anything until the police arrived.

Doc Cline's office had taken the body away a couple of hours earlier. The crime unit had worked all night in the artificial light, collecting footprints, tire treads and fiber samples, but hundreds of people used the recreational path every day, and the three boys who'd discovered Castleberry's body had contaminated the scene as well. The small bloody footprints were almost certainly Jason McLeod's. An area of matted grass beside the body indicated the killer might have lain in wait for his victim, but the techs came up empty when they combed the spot for evidence.

Bill moved among the technicians and officers, handing out doughnuts and coffee in foam cups. As I drank the hot liquid, I glimpsed a familiar face behind the crime tape where the trail intersected Windward Lane. Karen Englewood, dressed in a warm-up suit in vivid neon colors, waved at me, and I walked down the path toward her.

"I jog here every morning," she said. "The early news said there'd been a murder last night, but they didn't give a name."

"We're trying to track down the victim's mother before releasing the name to the press. Maybe you can help?"

"Me?" Her face paled and her legs began to buckle. "Oh, no. Not Larry?"

I shook my head. "Peter Castleberry."

"My God."

I slipped under the tape, grabbed her arm and led her to my car. When I opened the door, she collapsed on the front seat, gasping air through her gaping mouth like a fish out of water.

I waited until her breathing eased. "Does the clinic list next-of-kin in its records?"

"The office is closed on Saturdays," she said, "but I can run down and pull his mother's name and address from his medical file for you."

"The sooner, the better, so I can break the news before the media."

"I'll go right away." She started to rise, but I shook my head, and she sank back onto the car's seat.

"Castleberry was a long way from home," I said. "Any idea what he was doing here?"

"He exercised to speed up his weight loss, rode his bike ten miles on the trail every night. He'd load it in his van, drive to Dunedin, unload it, then ride to Clearwater and back, every night without fail."

"Why at night? The trail closes at sundown."

Karen's eyes filled with tears. "He couldn't stand the

ridicule, the taunting, when he rode in daylight. All the trim young jocks in spandex who laughed at him. He said he'd rather take his chances at being mugged than endure their insults."

I reached past her for the Benadryl container in the glove compartment. "Last night he suffered the ultimate insult."

"Poison again?"

"We're not releasing cause of death yet." I shucked off my jacket and rubbed gel into my itching arms. "Who else knew about his exercise routine?"

"Everybody at the clinic. He talked about it to the support group. We tried to discourage him from using the trail at night, but we understood his reasons."

"Did Castleberry ever mention any enemies?"

"He had a personality that antagonized everybody he met. It was a defense mechanism, his way of rejecting people before they rejected him. I don't know about enemies, but he didn't have any friends." Her color had returned and she pulled herself to her feet. "Do you think it was the same one?"

"The same one?"

"The same person who killed Edith and Sophia?"

"It's too soon to say. What do you think?"

Karen shivered in the morning chill and pulled her

jacket tighter around her. "I think everyone connected with the clinic better watch their backs."

"Where were you last night, between seven and ten?"

Her head jerked as if I'd slapped her. "At home."

"Alone?"

"Yes." Fear blossomed in her eyes.

"And Larry?"

"I...I haven't seen him since he stormed out of the house the evening you had supper with me."

"Any idea where he is?"

"Probably staying with one of the guys he hangs out with. I can get you the names."

In a lapse of objectivity, I felt sorry for her. "That would help."

I headed back toward the crime scene. The sun had cleared the treetops, and an object, partially hidden by a clump of wildflowers beneath a hedge at the far end of the clearing, caught my eye. A clear plastic, two-liter bottle protruded from the orange-and-yellow flowers. Its bottom was shattered, its spout wrapped in duct tape. I called to Adler to bring an evidence bag.

"What have you got?" he asked.

With my pen in the spout, I scooped up the bottle.

"A homemade silencer. This explains why the neighbors didn't hear the shot."

"You think this was another clinic murder, or was Castleberry merely in the wrong place at the wrong time?"

"The MO's different, but maybe the killer was afraid the others would be on guard against poison after what happened to Edith and Sophia." I handed the bag to a technician and made a note of where I'd found it. "If it's the same killer, he's given us a break."

"How do you figure?"

"Using poison, the killer could have been miles away when Edith and Sophia died. A gun is up close and personal. I'll find out where Tillett, Dorman, Morelli and Anastasia Gianakis were between sundown and ten last night. You check out the clinic staff and other patients."

"It's going to be a long day," Adler said. "I'd better get started." He ambled down the trail toward his SUV parked on Windward.

I watched him go, and strong hands grasped my shoulders from behind and began to massage the muscles there and in my neck.

"You've been up all night," Bill said, "and you were tired before all this went down. Go home and grab a few winks before you tackle those interviews."

I turned and stepped out of reach of his soothing hands. Much more of that kind of attention, and I'd wish his marriage proposals were serious. "You've been here all night, too. What's your read on this?"

"An execution-style killing, very different from poison. Could be a different killer, or the same one trying to throw investigators off balance. But if Castleberry's killer also killed Edith and Sophia, what's the motive?"

Fatigue seeped through me like biting cold. "Maybe Karen Englewood's right, and the killer is someone with a pathological hatred of fat people. What if someone unconnected to the clinic simply sought its patients out in his quest for victims?"

Bill threw his arm around my shoulder and guided me toward my car. "Don't try to reason in the shape you're in. After you drive me home, get some sleep. Being rested will save you time in the long run."

My phone was ringing when I arrived home.

"Margaret," my mother said when I answered, "where have you been? I tried to reach you before you left for work."

"I've been working all night, Mother."

"But I've been calling you for days." Her voice rang with accusation, as if I'd been purposely avoiding her.

"I have an answering machine. If you'd left a message, I'd have called you back."

A delicate sniff filtered through the line. "Such a vulgar practice, answering machines. I wanted to thank you for the book on Monet. It was very sweet of you, dear."

Mother was in an approving and expansive mood, and I was too dead on my feet to enjoy it. "I'm glad you like it, but I have to get some sleep. Can I call you later?"

"No need. Just pencil in dinner at the club Monday on your social calendar. Cedric has agreed to join us again."

Social calendar? She had to be kidding. And I didn't have the heart to tell her Cedric was on the make for lusty young waiters. "I can't promise. Work is keeping me busy."

"I've told you before, Margaret, if you'll just give up that dirty, common job, I'll set up a trust fund. You won't have to work at all."

For the first time in my life, I was tempted. Bone-tired and grimy, I stood in the early morning light in my unfamiliar kitchen. Peter Castleberry's shattered face was etched in my brain and his blood stained my shoes. Thoughts of full nights of sleep with no worries about serial killers or juveniles on a one-way track to perdition lured me to accept her offer.

"Think about it, darling," she said. "We could see so much more of each other."

Temptation vanished. I said goodbye and hung up. Too weary to climb the stairs, I stretched out on the living room sofa and fell asleep. After what seemed only minutes, my beeper sounded and I stumbled to the phone to call the medical examiner's office. A glance at the clock told me I'd been asleep less than an hour.

"Your shooter used a .22," Doris Cline said, "and fragments of clear plastic are embedded in the entry wound."

"That fits with the homemade silencer I found. Anything else?"

"No signs of struggle. The killer probably came up behind him and fired, caught him completely by surprise. Death was instantaneous."

I hung up and headed for the shower. When I'd bathed and dressed in beige slacks and an ivory blouse, my beeper sounded again.

Kyle Dayton answered the phone at the station. "Ms. Englewood left you a message. Says Castleberry's mother is Esther Truett."

I scribbled the address. Dreading the task ahead, I headed for Largo to inform a mother that her son was dead.

CHAPTER 15

Esther Truett lived in a mobile home park off East Bay Drive. I turned at the park's clubhouse and winded my way through dozens of aluminum houses, disasters waiting to happen when a major hurricane, long overdue in the Tampa Bay area, finally struck. The single-wides were packed cheek by jowl on narrow lots. A resident could sit in his kitchen and watch his neighbor cook supper.

At Number 112, I parked in the driveway behind an aging Chevy. A row of terra-cotta pots in various sizes, filled with scraggly plants, a pathetic excuse for a garden, edged the carport. I rapped on a jalousie pane of the front door.

A tall, raw-boned woman with steel-gray hair in a Dutch-boy cut answered the door. She buttoned the jacket of her lavender polyester pantsuit and picked up a worn Bible from the table as if she was going out.

"Esther Truett?" I showed my identification and introduced myself.

"What is it? I'm late for my Bible class already." She made no effort to keep the impatience from her voice.

"I have some information about your son. May I come in?"

"No time. What do you want?"

"It's bad news, Mrs. Truett."

"Has he been arrested? I'm not surprised. I raised him in a good Christian home, never spared the rod, but the Devil got his hands on him. All my prayers couldn't save him."

"Your son is dead. I'm sorry."

I waited for the look of shock, the tears, but the angry set of the woman's strong jaw never wavered.

"It's the Lord's judgment," she said, "to chastise him for his sins."

"Can we go inside? Your son was murdered, and I need to ask you some questions."

She heaved a sigh of exasperation and stood aside. "If there's no getting around it, come in."

She faced me with her Bible gripped tightly in both hands, but she didn't offer me a seat. I glanced around the compact living room of faded upholstered furniture, capped with crocheted doilies. A huge portrait of

Christ painted on black velvet hung above a patterned sofa, but no pictures of her son were visible anywhere in the room.

I turned back to Esther. "You said Peter was killed for his sins. Was he in some kind of trouble?"

"The worst kind. The threat of hellfire."

"Why?"

"Deadly sins, gluttony and sloth. And failure to honor his father."

I surveyed the adjoining kitchen and empty hall. "Is his father here?"

"Dead, since Peter was a baby."

"Then how—"

"Samuel Truett married me when Peter was two, raised Peter like his own son. That man was the salt of the earth. Beat Peter for his own good when his feet strayed from the path, but the boy had no righteousness in his heart. He hated Sam for it. Didn't even come to his funeral two years ago."

"When did you last see your son?"

"Before Sam died. When Peter failed to pay his final respects, I disowned him, but I still pray night and day for his eternal soul."

"Can you think of any reason someone wanted to kill him?"

"An agent of the Lord, wreaking God's vengeance."

The woman gave me the willies. "Any idea who that agent might be?"

She shook her head. "The Lord moves in mysterious ways."

"He didn't happen to have any help from you, did he?"

Her nostrils flared. "How can you say such a thing?"

"Biblical precedent?"

"I will pray for you, Detective Skerritt. Blasphemers are doomed to burn in hell."

Unfortunately, I supposed every religion had its fanatics. "Aren't you even curious how Peter died? Whether he was alone, frightened? If he asked for you?"

Her jaw relaxed, her eyes grew moist, and for a moment, I believed she was human after all. Then she gripped the Bible tighter. "As far as I'm concerned, my son died a long time ago."

I choked back my disgust. "Here's where you can claim the body."

I scribbled the telephone number of the medical examiner's office on the back of my card, laid it on the desk beside the door and left before I blurted my opinion of her. I hoped Castleberry had made it to heaven. His mother had already put him through hell on earth.

* * *

The stiff sea breezes on the terrace at Sophia's lifted my hair away from the new blotches on my face, the product of my encounter with Esther Truett. I downed another cup of coffee and struggled to keep alert while my body screamed for sleep.

"Detective Skerritt." Lester Morelli stood beside me, his body blocking the midmorning sun. "I wanted to thank you."

"Thank me?"

He slid onto the chair across from me. "For being at Sophia's service yesterday. That was kind of you."

The skin on his face appeared drawn too tight over his cheekbones and bags puffed beneath his eyes. When the waitress approached, he ordered a Bloody Mary.

"Hair of the dog," he explained. "Have you found the bastard who killed my wife?"

"There's been another murder."

"Jesus." His hands shook as he reached in the pocket of his golf shirt and withdrew a pack of cigarettes. "Who?"

"Peter Castleberry."

He struck a match from a book with Sophia's embossed in gold letters and lit his cigarette. "That's a shame. Castleberry wasn't a likable man, but he had a great talent. Didn't someone warn him about the vitamins?"

"Vitamins?"

"Poison. I thought you warned the other patients after what happened to Sophia."

"Castleberry wasn't poisoned."

Morelli drew deeply on his cigarette, then exhaled through his nose. Smoke swirled on the morning breeze. The waitress placed his drink before him, and he removed a leafy stalk of celery before taking a long swallow.

"What's going on, Detective?"

"There're a number of possibilities."

A trace of a smile scudded across his face. "You mean suspects?"

"Where were you last night between sunset and ten?"

"And it seems I'm one of them." He took another drag on his cigarette, then crushed it in a crystal ashtray. "After the funeral yesterday, I gave a luncheon here for Sophia's relatives and close friends. When it was over, I drove two of her cousins to the airport. I couldn't face my empty house, so I came back here."

"What time did you leave last night?"

"I don't know."

"You aren't sure?"

"I don't know. I went to my office when I returned from the airport and had a few drinks. The next thing I knew, I woke up in my bed early today at home. I didn't know how I got there until I talked with Antonio this morning. He says he drove me home after the restaurant closed, sometime after midnight."

Morelli was taking his wife's death hard. Between cigarettes and alcohol, he'd soon join her if he didn't get a grip.

I remembered his confrontation with Sophia's aunt at the graveside. "Was Anastasia Gianakis at the luncheon yesterday?"

His face twisted with distaste. "That crazy old bat. I invited her, but she's convinced herself I'm the one who killed Sophia. Claims I did it for the money, that Sophia was about to leave me. She left me, all right."

Tears flooded his eyes. He finished his drink and signaled the waitress for another.

"Why would Anastasia make such claims?" I asked.

"She wants Sophia's money so bad, she can taste it. If she can get me out of the picture, it's all hers."

"She threatened you?"

He shrugged. "She's offensive, but harmless."

"You don't think she had a hand in Sophia's death?"

He looked surprised. "She did visit the house two days before Sophia died. Sophia wanted to believe her aunt loved her, but I always felt the old woman was more attracted to the Gianakis fortune than her niece."

When the waitress brought his second drink, he rose from the table and took his Bloody Mary with him. "If you'll excuse me, I've neglected business this past week, and there are things I must take care of."

He walked back toward the building with his shoulders hunched, as if a great weight bore down on him. Antonio met him at the door, and the two exchanged words. When Morelli stepped inside, Antonio hurried to my table. "Mr. Morelli said you had some questions."

The maître d' confirmed that Morelli had been in his office from around five-thirty until after midnight the previous night, consuming another bottle of Jack Daniel's. Antonio had taken him home and put him to bed.

"What about Dorman?" I asked. "Did he work last night?"

"We were closed to the public at noon, but Brent worked the luncheon for the funeral guests. After he cleared up from lunch, his back was bothering him again, so he left."

"Is he in today?"

Antonio nodded. "He brought Mr. Morelli to work, since his car is still here from yesterday. I'll send him to you."

"Don't bother. I'll find him."

I passed through the empty main dining room and into the spacious lobby. On my right, a hall led past restrooms to Morelli's office. The door stood ajar, and Lester sat behind his desk, punching keys on an adding machine.

To my left, large swinging doors opened into the kitchen, where the staff was preparing lunch. A blast of spice-laden steam hit me as I entered the room. A man wearing the short white cap of a sous chef approached, and I asked for Dorman.

"He's on break, out back." He pointed to a rear entrance.

I found Dorman doing push-ups behind a row of Dumpsters and overflowing garbage cans. "Pretty good for a guy with a bad back."

He jumped to his feet and dusted his hands on the sides of his slacks. "As a matter of fact, exercise helps tone the back muscles. You should try it sometime."

"Where did you go yesterday afternoon after you left the restaurant?"

One corner of his mouth lifted in a sneer. "Still

haven't caught your killer, eh, Detective? Maybe if they had a man on the job, they'd get better results."

I resisted the urge to ram the heel of my palm up his snotty little nose. "Glad to know you're an equal-opportunity bigot, Dorman. Do you want to answer my question here, or would you rather go down to the station for a cozy chat?"

"I got nothing to hide. I went to the Body Shop for another massage, then home. Spent the evening watching television."

"Didn't happen to take a run on the trail after supper?"

"The trail closes at dark. I run in the mornings before I work out at the gym, so I turn in early. Went to bed last night, right after watching *JAG*."

"Alone?"

"What is this? You get your thrills from poking into other people's sex lives? Yeah, sorry to disappoint you, but I was alone."

"Do you remember Peter Castleberry?"

He wrinkled his nose in obvious dislike. "Wish I could forget. He's a blimp and a crybaby. Squealed like a stuck pig every time I drew his blood. Complained I hurt him on purpose. I couldn't stand the sight or the smell of the guy."

"And no one can vouch that you were at home all evening?"

"What is this?" His eyes narrowed. "Another fatso bite the dust?"

"Sorry to see you so broken up about it." I pivoted on my heel, disgusted, then turned back. "There's one muscle in that finely tuned physique of yours in serious need of development, Dorman."

"Yeah, what's that?"

"Your heart." I left him standing alone among the garbage, where he belonged.

Stephanie Tillett answered my telephone call and told me her husband was playing his Saturday round of golf at the country club. I left Sophia's and drove north, but instead of turning west into Pelican Point where Morelli lived, I headed east toward Osprey Lake.

The long, low clubhouse of the Osprey Country Club sprawled on the lake's western shore with an Olympic-size swimming pool on one end and a pro shop and golf-cart garages on the other, flanking the central dining rooms and bar. The sounds of kids cannonballing off the pool's diving board drifted across the grounds as I left my car. When I reached the pro shop, I learned Tillett would be finishing his round soon and that he always reported afterward to the nineteenth hole.

I wandered toward the bar to wait, but a formidable man in a black suit blocked my way. He gazed down his aquiline nose from a distinguished height. "This club is for members only."

I had reached in my pocket for my badge when a hand grasped my elbow.

"This lady's with me." Chief Shelton guided me to a table in the corner. "What the hell are you doing here, Skerritt? We've had the third murder in a week. You should be on the street, tracking down a killer."

"That's why I'm here."

"You think the killer belongs to this club?" He looked as if I'd just alleged that the pope was an atheist.

"I didn't say that. Richard Tillett's a member here. His patients are rapidly turning up dead. I have a few more questions for him, that's all."

Shelton leaned across the table and hissed in a low voice, "Dammit, Skerritt, you've got to be more discreet. The man has a reputation to uphold."

"Not if his patients keep dropping like flies. What do you want me to do, Chief? Sit at the station and twiddle my thumbs until I can question him in the privacy of his home?"

"What's wrong with that?"

"Time, and time is running out. When I started this case, I had a list with seven names, one of them dead. Now three are dead, there're four names left, and they're all Tillett's patients."

"Okay, but keep it low-key, will you?"

For a man dressed in fire-engine red slacks and a green-and-red-checked shirt, he had a lot of nerve asking me to tone it down. "I'll be the picture of propriety."

Tillett and three other men appeared in the doorway to the bar. The chief laid a restraining hand on my arm, then jumped up and strode across the room. He returned with Tillett in tow. "I'll leave you two. I'm sure the detective won't take much of your time, Rich."

Tillett took the chair the chief had vacated. "George said you wanted to bring me up to speed on the Wainwright and Morelli murders. Can I buy you a drink?"

"Too early in the day for me, thanks. Have you heard the morning news?"

"I overslept and just made my tee-off time." He seemed more at ease than he'd been a week ago.

"There's been another murder."

He stiffened and his smile faded. "Who?"

"Peter Castleberry."

"Bloody hell." Fear flared in his pale blue eyes. "How?"

"The important question is when. Last night between seven and ten. Where were you during that time?"

Fear expanded into panic. His rate of breathing increased, and his glance flicked around the room, as if searching for an escape route. "I don't have an alibi."

"You had to be somewhere."

"At the office."

"Alone?"

"Paperwork. What with insurance and Medicare, I'm never caught up. I worked from six until almost midnight."

My beeper sounded. I looked around for a phone and saw the chief glaring at me from the bar. "I'll be in touch, Dr. Tillett."

When I telephoned the station, the dispatcher passed on the name of an informant who wanted to talk about a car-theft ring and a possible chop shop operating in our area. I made a note of the information and hurried out of the clubhouse before the chief could collar me again.

While I was on the north side of town, I drove up Alternate U.S. 19, through Dunedin and Palm Harbor to Tarpon Springs, intending to meet Anastasia Gianakis and ask a few questions. She had a motive for Sophia's murder, and although her connections to Edith and Peter were tenuous, they placed her in the pool of suspects. I checked both her house and her gift shop near the sponge docks but she was at neither, and no one could tell me where to find her. I returned to her house and tucked my card in her front door with a note to contact me.

Rather than sit around waiting for Anastasia to call, I spent the late afternoon and most of the evening tracking down a scuzzball named Ross Hubert in Oldsmar. When I found him at a pub on Race Track Road, he wanted money but didn't have any information worth buying. It was after ten that night when I drove back to the station. Adler was at his desk, filling out reports.

"Your little girl's going to forget what her daddy looks like," I said.

"Uh-uh. My wife's a genius. She filmed a video of me, talking to Jessica, telling her stories. When I have to work long hours, Sharon plays it constantly. Says it keeps both of them company."

And it would be a tangible memory if her policeman father were killed in the line of duty. I wondered how many other officers' families had made such films, making a stab at immortality, a tiny hedge against loss.

"Any luck with Tillett's staff?" I asked.

He swiveled in his chair and leaned back with his fingers locked behind his head. "Their alibis are airtight, except for Gale Whatley, the office manager. Says she was home alone with no one to verify it. How 'bout you?"

"Morelli was too sloshed to walk a straight line, much less commit murder, but Dorman and Tillett lack alibis. Dorman has the cold-bloodedness to have done it, and something has Tillett running scared, but I can't press charges based on bigotry or fear. So where does that leave us?"

Adler kicked one foot, rotating his chair. "Same place as yesterday, with one exception."

I turned on my computer monitor, pulled up a blank report and turned up the squelch on the scanner on my desk. "What exception?"

"We can scratch Peter Castleberry as a suspect."

"Talk about explicating the blooming obvi—" I stopped at the sound of Darcy's voice on the radio.

"—breaking and entering in progress at 10 Windward Lane. Complainant is locked in her bedroom. Says someone just smashed the glass on her front door."

I sprang to my feet. "Let's roll. That's Karen Englewood's house."

CHAPTER 16

Adler reached under the seat of my Volvo for my emergency light.

"Leave it," I said. "This may be our killer, and I don't want to scare him off."

Few cars roamed the streets of Pelican Bay on a Saturday night, and we met no traffic obstacles as we sped the few short blocks down Edgewater. When I turned onto Windward, I cut my headlights and pulled across the street from Karen's. Her house and those of her neighbors were dark. In the distance a siren wailed, a green-and-white en route.

I keyed my radio. "You still have the complainant on the line?"

"Ten-four," Darcy said.

"Tell her we're on the scene, to keep her door locked, and not to come out until I say so."

I turned to Adler. "You take the back. I'll go in the front."

I grabbed my flashlight, climbed out of the car and eased the door shut without a sound. Adler disappeared at a loping run around the corner of the house, and I approached the front door at an angle to avoid the walkway bathed in the yellow glow of the streetlight. Under cover of a pittosporum hedge, I edged my way toward the porch. I could hear nothing but the approaching siren and the hiss of my own breathing.

I crept up the front steps toward the door. Shards of glass, broken from the glass panel on the door's right side, covered the porch floor. The door stood ajar with the lock unforced. The intruder had simply reached through the opening in the broken panel and unlocked it.

A patrol car pulled up and squelched its siren. Steve Johnson barreled up the steps, hand on his gun and stopped beside me.

"We'll make a sweep of the house," I said in a whisper. "Adler's around back. When we've cleared the downstairs, we'll let him in and the two of you can check the second floor."

"You think our guy's still in there?"

"If he is, he isn't making any noise. Ready?"

Johnson kicked the door open and stepped in. We quickly progressed through the rooms, turned on lights, checked closets and behind draperies. When we reached the kitchen, I unlocked the door for Adler and the two men headed upstairs. They returned a few minutes later with Karen.

"You okay?" I asked.

She dropped into a chair at the table and managed a weak smile. "I feel like a James Bond martini, shaken, not stirred."

Adler and Johnson left us to search the lawn and shrubbery. I sat across from Karen. "What happened?"

"I was reading in bed and had just turned out the light when I heard glass breaking downstairs. I always sleep with my bedroom door locked. I learned that through the Neighborhood Watch program. I used my bedside phone to call 911. The operator kept me on the line until the officers reached my door and told me it was safe to come out."

"Did you hear anything before the glass broke? The sound of a vehicle, a car door slamming?" If the burglar had wheels, he was long gone by now.

"Nothing. Everything was quiet until then." She tugged a velour robe closer around her and tightened its sash. "But whoever broke in made a heck of a racket. I'm afraid to look at the damage."

"You'll have to, to tell us what's missing."

She set her mouth in a tight line. "Let's get it over with."

I followed her up the hall into the living room and heard her sharp intake of breath at the shambles before her. A coffee table was overturned and drawers of end tables wrenched out, but she found nothing missing. We crossed the hall into her study, a book-lined room with a large mahogany desk as the centerpiece. Books had been raked from the shelves, and a brass lamp, its shade crushed, lay on its side on the desk. The drawers gaped open.

"Don't touch anything," I said. "Just look. We'll want to dust for prints."

"Nothing's been taken." She pointed to a collection of silver candlesticks, a stereo system and a DVD player. "Wouldn't the thief have grabbed something to make the break-in worth his while?"

"Could Larry have done this?"

She shook her head. "He has a key. If he wanted something, he would have just walked in and taken it."

"One of his friends?"

"It's possible. More than one of them has a drug habit to support. But if that's the case, why didn't they steal anything?"

Adler appeared in the doorway. "Nothing outside."

"Request a K-9 unit," I told him, "and get the techs over here."

"On my way." He disappeared again.

"Isn't that a lot of bother for a common thief—" Karen's eyes grew round as she faced me. "It wasn't a common thief, was it? You think it's the person who's been killing Dr. Tillett's patients."

"Maybe you could make us a pot of coffee," I said. "It's going to be a long night."

"Three of my clients are dead, Detective. It isn't beyond the realm of possibility that whoever killed them might want me dead, too."

"The realm of possibility is a helluva big territory. You can drive yourself crazy trying to cover it all."

"My God, we can't have that. A crazy psychologist?" With a laugh that bordered on hysteria, she headed for the kitchen.

Johnson ambled into the front hallway. "Anything missing?"

"Zip. Looks like someone threw a tantrum and ran away empty-handed." I mentally cataloged a number of valuable items a thief could have carted away under one arm. "We were here fast, but not that fast. He had time to pull a profit."

Johnson stood with his hands on his hips and surveyed

the scene. "Reminds me of a break-in call on the east side I answered about six months ago. Guy's darkroom—"

"Darkroom?"

"Yeah, turned inside out, but nothing taken. Belonged to Castleberry, same guy who was stiffed last night on the trail."

"Any of his developing chemicals stolen?"

"Said he'd take an inventory, and if anything turned up missing, he'd let me know. I never heard from him."

"Why didn't you tell me this when we found Castleberry's body?"

Johnson had the sense to look chagrined. "Sorry. I'd forgotten all about it till now."

And Johnson wondered why he'd never made detective. I suppressed a sigh.

Out front, a vehicle pulled up and a dog barked. Johnson peeked out the curtains toward the street. "K-9 unit's here. I'll see if they need a hand."

My head was whirling. Six months earlier someone had broken into Castleberry's darkroom. If Peter had discovered a jar of potassium ferricyanide crystals missing, would he have reported it or simply purchased a new one? I'd ask Bill to check with Castleberry's supplier for dates of purchases.

Karen padded in from the kitchen with a large wooden tray bearing a coffeepot and several mugs.

"Do you keep any clinic files here?" I asked.

She handed me a mug steaming with coffee. "Everything's in my office at the clinic. Why?"

"Still trekking the realm of endless possibilities."

A crime-scene technical team arrived and unloaded equipment in the front hall.

"Why don't we wait in the kitchen, out of the way?" I said to Karen. "This could take a while."

We sat at the big kitchen table again, and as I sipped coffee, Karen picked at the frayed end of the sash of her robe.

"You sure this has nothing to do with Larry?" I said.

"Four years ago, I'd have been sure. He's changed so much since I divorced his father, I'm not sure about anything that concerns him now."

"I'd better have a talk with him. Can you get me those names you mentioned this morning?"

"This morning?" She looked blank. "Oh, on the trail. My God, that already seems like years ago."

Moving like an old woman, she levered herself from her chair and shuffled across to the island, where she removed a pad and pencil from the drawer. She returned to her chair, wrote three names and handed me the paper. "They live somewhere in North Clearwater. That's all I know about them."

An hour later, Adler returned to the kitchen. "K-9 unit picked up a scent on the porch, followed it to Edgewater and up along the waterfront, but lost it in the marina park."

"Any footprints or trace evidence outside?" I asked, but wasn't hopeful. Unlike the popular CSI crime dramas would have us believe, criminals weren't always so cooperative or unlucky in leaving incriminating evidence behind.

"Nope," Adler said, "but we'll check again at daylight. It's my guess this guy sashayed up the front walk, then left the same way, judging by the route the K-9 traced, but none of the neighbors saw anything. They were all asleep until the siren wakened them."

"Are the techs finished?"

"Almost. Johnson's going to drop me off at the station to get my car, so you don't have to drive me back." He headed toward the front of the house with Johnson at his heels.

Karen filled my cup from a fresh pot. "Can I give you something to eat?"

"No, I—"

"We're through, Detective." Susie, the younger of the tech team, stood in the doorway.

"What have you got?"

"A few good sets of prints. We'll have to check them against Ms. Englewood's and her son's. Nothing else out of the ordinary…"

Her inflection hinted otherwise. "Except what?"

"Just seems strange the burglar didn't take the gun," she said.

"What gun?" Karen asked. "I don't have a gun."

"There's a gun in your top desk drawer," Susie said.

"Could it be Larry's?" I asked.

Karen shook her head. "There is no gun."

"Look, lady, it's late," Susie said, "and I'm too tired to argue. Come see for yourself."

I hurried up the hall and into Karen's study. Shoved to the back and barely visible in the partially opened drawer was the butt of a handgun.

"It's a gun, all right," I said to Karen. "Do I have your permission to examine it?"

"Why do you need my permission? It's not my gun." The note of hysteria had returned to her voice. "Go ahead. Examine it. Take it with you."

I slipped a pencil through the trigger guard, lifted the weapon from the drawer and placed it on a blotter beneath the desk lamp. A blued .22 automatic. "Don't leave yet, Susie. I want this checked for prints, then handed over to ballistics."

"How did it get there?" Karen's hands trembled as she clutched the collar of her robe closed at her throat.

I lifted a narrow remnant of duct tape trailing off the barrel. "If I knew that, I'd know who killed Peter Castleberry."

CHAPTER 17

Bill was still awake, watching the final minutes of the *One O'Clock Movie* when I rapped on the window of his boat and climbed aboard.

"I need your help," I said when he slid open the door to the cabin.

"You got it. Want coffee?"

"No, thanks. I'm on such a caffeine high right now, I won't stop shaking for a week." I sprawled on his tiny sofa and kicked off my shoes.

"You need sleep."

"Can't. Too damn busy." I told him what Adler and I had learned from the day's interviews and about the gun discovered at Karen Englewood's. "I can't make sense of any of it."

"Sleep deprivation makes it hard to think. I've got just the ticket."

He took a saucepan from a galley cabinet, filled it

with milk and turned on a burner. In a few minutes, I was sipping hot chocolate and eating homemade oatmeal cookies.

"Comfort food," he said.

"Were you a Jewish mother in a former life?" The food worked its magic, melting away my caffeine jitters.

"A good Jewish mother would insist you give up this job and take better care of yourself."

I reached for another cookie. "Can't. Have to find a killer."

"Why you? Adler's a good man. Resign and let him handle the case."

I leaned back against the cushions. "When Greg was murdered in the emergency room, his death threw my entire life into chaos. I was a spoiled rich brat who never thought past what dress to wear to the next club dance. When that crack addict pumped five bullets into him at close range, my eyes were opened to the disorder and destruction in the world. I can't fix the entire world, but I can make my little corner of it a better place. In this case, that means taking a serial killer out of circulation."

Bill slipped his arms around my shoulders and pulled me closer, pressing me against his warm, reassuring bulk. "You're a wonder, Margaret. A cop for more than twenty years, and still an idealist."

I snuggled closer. "It's a nasty job, but somebody's got to do it."

"Not only nasty, it's unending. You nab this guy, another takes his place. When do you say, 'enough'?"

"Not yet. I'll know when the time's right." I couldn't keep my eyes open. The last thing I remembered was his removing the mug from my grip.

I dreamed. The sky curved overhead, and suddenly patches of blue flaked away like falling plaster, revealing water-soaked laths. "Tsunami," a voice whispered, and the wave came, lifting me off my feet. The crest of the comber carried me away, and I struggled to regain my footing.

Still rocking on the wave, I opened my eyes. I lay in the wide double bed in Bill's cabin with the sun peeking through the curtains. My body felt rested, but feelings of doom and frustration lingered from my strange dream.

"Breakfast is ready," Bill called from the galley. "But there's time for a shower if you like."

I used the tiny toilet in the head, washed my face in the midget-size sink and brushed my teeth with a finger and Bill's toothpaste, banging my elbows on the bulkhead in the process.

When I scooted onto the bench in the dining nook, Bill poured dollops of batter onto a hot griddle. I dug into a compote of mangoes and sliced bananas sprinkled with lime juice. When I finished, Bill placed a stack of pancakes and a bottle of blueberry syrup at my place.

"I can't eat all that."

"Sure you can." He drizzled syrup over his own jumbo stack. "You have work to do, and work takes energy."

"Maybe I should burn some of the energy from my bulging thighs instead."

"There's nothing wrong with your thighs." He wiggled his eyebrows and grinned. "This case has made you oversensitive."

"That, too. My hives still flare up at least once a day."

"Last night you said you needed my help. What do you want me to do?"

"It's time to put a few of our suspects under surveillance. If Adler and I juggle Dorman between us, will you tail Tillett for me?"

"Sure. But what about Karen Englewood? She's connected to all the victims, the last murder took place a couple blocks from her house, and what could be the murder weapon was found in her desk. Does she have an alibi for the night Castleberry was shot?"

I shook my head. "But what's her motive? She cares about these people."

"Does she? Or is that what she wants you to believe?"

I set down my fork. "What makes you say that?"

"This killer, whoever it is, is a sadistic bastard, playing with your head, switching MOs, planting the gun and staging a break-in for you to find it."

"If Karen's the killer, it doesn't make sense for her to plant a gun to implicate herself."

Bill smiled and wiped a drip of syrup off his chin. "Exactly what she'd want you to think."

I remembered the card I'd found at Edith's house with Karen's name typed on it. Had it been dropped accidentally or left on purpose? "Are you saying she should be tailed instead of Tillett?"

"If you had the necessary manpower for this case, you'd tail 'em all. But I doubt you can make a tightwad like Councilman Ulrich understand that."

"Start with Tillett for now," I said.

"Give me his address. I'll begin right after breakfast. What about Morelli?"

"Adler and I can keep tabs on him while we watch Dorman. According to the maître d', Morelli spends most of his time three sheets to the wind in his office at the restaurant. My project *du jour* is Larry Englewood. He hates his mother's clients, hangs out on a spoil island near Morelli's house, and could be the one who stashed the gun at his mother's place and made it look like a break-in."

Bill pointed to my plate. "First, your breakfast. It's getting cold."

I took a bite of pancake that melted on my tongue. "God, Malcolm, is there anything you *can't* do?"

He gave me a funny look. "Yeah. Convince you to marry me."

I laughed, but my heart skipped a beat.

None of the three names Karen gave me were listed in the telephone directory, but when I called the Clearwater PD, the desk sergeant gave me the same address for all three. Each had priors for narcotics possession, petty larceny, and drunk and disorderly.

Sunday boaters crowded the channel as I drove along the waterfront toward Clearwater. Where the road curved inland, away from the water's edge, urban blight began. I found the address I was looking for on the west side of North Fort Harrison Avenue, a once-grand two-story house built in the 1920s, now run-down and converted into apartments. Its peeling coat of Bermuda coral paint did little to brighten its curb appeal.

Larry's Trans Am was parked around back, and I

climbed the iron outdoor staircase to reach the apartment number listed on the address. I knocked at the door several minutes before a young man with his face half hidden by an unruly mop of black hair answered. He tucked a thick strand behind one ear and stared at me with dilated pupils. "What?"

"I'm not selling Avon." I displayed my badge. "Detective Skerritt, Pelican Bay Police—"

The room behind him erupted into a cacophony of curses and moving bodies. Deep in the apartment's interior, a toilet flushed. The kid at the door glanced uneasily over his shoulder at the activity.

I paused, waiting until the toilet had flushed once more and hoping more illegal drugs had vanished down the tubes, before I continued. "I'm looking for Larry Englewood."

The kid at the door looked past me to Larry's car parked behind the house, and I wondered if the apartment had a rear door. From the dilapidated look of the fire-trap of a building, I doubted it.

"You got a warrant?" he said.

"No. There was trouble at his mother's place last night, and I want to talk to him about it."

Larry appeared and pushed the kid out of the way. "Mom, is she okay?"

The odor of stale beer, unwashed bodies and pot drifted through the open door, and I almost tossed Bill's gourmet pancakes. "Your mom's fine, just shaken up. Can we talk somewhere else?"

He pulled the door closed behind him and pointed down the street that ran alongside the house to the bay. "There's a dock where Ace and Stuey keep their boat. We can walk down there."

I followed him down the stairs, then fell in step beside him. He looked younger than the first time I saw him, more vulnerable without the anger that had hardened his face. "Where were you last night?"

"What happened to Mom?"

"You answer my questions, I'll answer yours."

He shoved his hands in his back pockets, and I lengthened my stride to keep up with his long-legged gait.

"Ace, Stuey and I were on the spoil bank. Spent most of the night there."

"Doing what?"

"Just hanging, drinking beer. That's not illegal, is it?" He attempted surliness but came across scared.

"Not if that's all you did."

We walked onto the wooden pier where a white outboard was moored. I tested the sturdiness of the wooden railing, then leaned against it and watched the young man at my side. His clothes looked as if he'd slept in them, and although he'd pulled his long hair back and tied it at his neck, its snarls and tangles hadn't seen a comb in days. He looked weary, hungry and gaunt.

"Why don't you go home, Larry? Why stay in a place like that?" I pointed toward the apartment house that looked even more ramshackle and dangerous from the bayside.

"And have Mom on my back all the time? Forget it."

"What was she on you about?"

I expected him to mouth off about minding my own business, but he surprised me. He lowered himself to a sitting position on the dock, pulled off his Nikes and dipped his bare feet in the water.

"About getting a job, keeping decent hours, like I'm some little kid. No wonder my dad left her."

"A job and decent hours sound pretty grown-up to me. What's really bugging you?" Funny how sometimes folks will say things to a stranger they'll never admit to someone they know. Larry was no exception.

"Since my dad left, I never see him. If she hadn't asked him to leave, things would be different."

"Why did your folks split?"

"Mom said Dad was catting around. He denied it,

but he left. I haven't seen him since I was fifteen, and it's all her fault."

"How come? No visitation rights?"

"Yeah, he has 'em. She gave him everything he asked for, just to get rid of him."

"Then if he really wanted to see you, he could?"

He looked at me as if I'd hit him. "That's what Mom says."

"Maybe you're blaming the wrong person. Why don't you find your dad and talk to him, clear the air?"

He kicked his foot and splashed salty water over both of us. "When are you going to tell me what happened to my mom?"

"Do you own a gun?"

"Hell, no. Mom would freak if I brought a gun into the house. She's terrified of them."

"I have an eyewitness who puts you and one of your friends on the beach outside Sophia Morelli's house the day she was murdered." I was groping in the dark again, but sometimes I bumped up against my best leads that way. "What were you doing on Pelican Point at six in the morning that day?"

I'd hit the mark. Larry didn't move. Water lapped the pilings beneath the dock, and a seagull screeched overhead, but everything else was quiet in the October morning. I lifted my face to the sun and wished I hadn't left my sunglasses in the car.

When he finally spoke, his voice was soft, like a child's. "I don't remember much. We'd been—" He looked at me with anxious eyes. "We smoked pot all night. Stuey said it would be a kick to see how the other two percent live, so we took the boat over to Pelican Point. The water's the only way to get around the security guards."

"What did you do there?"

"Nothing, I swear it. We just walked up and down the beach, wondering how much money it took to live in houses like those. Then Stuey spots some old guy on a balcony, and we took off."

"Did you see anyone else? Notice anything unusual?"

"No, if you don't call living like royalty unusual." He rubbed his palms against his thighs, then crossed his arms over his chest. Fear softened his features, making him appear younger than his nineteen years. Unlike so many of the antisocial juveniles I'd dealt with, Larry obviously knew the difference between right and wrong and cared about the consequences. Somewhere along the way, his parents had done their job.

He squared his shoulders and lifted his chin. "Are you going to arrest me?"

I shook my head. "Three of your mother's clients have been murdered in the past week, the last one just two blocks from her house. And someone broke into her house last night."

He snapped his head around and stared at me. "You're sure she's okay? Nobody hurt her?"

I kneeled on the dock beside him and placed my hand on his shoulder. "Nobody's hurt her yet. But she may be in danger. She'd be safer if you were there."

He jerked away from my touch. "She doesn't want me."

"I wouldn't be so sure. Think about it."

I left him dangling his feet in the bay and returned to my car. I had a hell of a nerve offering advice to anyone on how to get along with his mother.

My beeper sounded as I headed north toward Pelican Bay. I spotted a pay phone at a convenience store, pulled in and dialed the station.

"Bill Malcolm left you a message," Darcy said. "Wants you to meet him in the hospital emergency room."

CHAPTER 18

The hospital's automatic doors shushed open, and I darted into the cool artificial light of the hall and the smell of antiseptic and recycled air. A perky young woman with a cheerleader smile looked up from a computer monitor at the reception desk.

"Bill Malcolm?" I asked.

She pointed down the hallway. "In the waiting room."

I spotted Bill, dressed in denim shorts and a T-shirt, sprawled on a vinyl sofa watching *Meet the Press* with about twenty other patients and their families. He jumped to his feet when he saw me.

"Thank God you're okay." I shoved away dark memories resurrected by the ER. "What are you doing here?"

"Following Tillett."

"Don't tell me another of his patients is dead," I hissed in his ear.

"It's not that simple." He glanced around the

crowded waiting room. "Let's go somewhere we can talk."

In the deserted corridor, I turned on him. "What gives?"

"After you left this morning, I drove to Tillett's house and parked up the street. Tillett's Infiniti was in the drive. After a while, Tillett comes out, gets into his car and drives off. I slid in behind him at a distance. Everything's fine until he hits the intersection at Orangewood and Main. The light's red, but he doesn't stop, doesn't even slow down, and a blue Bronco broadsides him."

"Injuries?"

"Driver of the Bronco was treated and released. Tillett's in one of the trauma rooms. Paramedics at the scene said he's got a broken arm. Would've been worse if he hadn't had air bags."

"Did the investigating officer question Tillett?"

"He swears his brakes failed."

"What do you think?" I scratched the back of my hands where welts had erupted with new vigor.

"Could be mechanical failure, an accident." He leaned above me, one hand braced on the wall. "Could be somebody fixed his brakes."

"Would you check with the garage where the car was towed? Find out if the brakes were tampered with." I hated to ask, but Adler was trailing Dorman, and I had to question Tillett.

Bill nodded. "There're a couple other possible explanations for Tillett's accident."

"Suicide attempt?"

"That, or a diversion. An accident he planned himself to make it look like someone was out to get him."

I considered the implications. If Tillett was a victim, or perceived as a victim, he'd knock himself off the list of suspects. "If the latter's true, he took a helluva chance."

Bill raised his eyebrows. "Desperate times—"

"I know, desperate measures. Maybe he did risk it. The man's a chronic gambler. Call me when you have some info on the brakes."

We walked toward the entrance. Bill marched straight out the doors, and I showed my badge to the receptionist. "I want to see Dr. Richard Tillett. EMS brought him in a while ago."

An ER nurse in blue scrubs led me to a cubicle in the trauma room and whisked aside a curtain. Tillett lay still and pale against the sheets, his head swathed in bandages, his left arm in a cast.

"Try not to excite him," the nurse said, "but don't let him drop off to sleep, either. We want him awake while we monitor his concussion."

She drew the curtain around us when she left, and I moved to his right side.

"Rough morning, Doctor?" I asked.

He shifted, tried to sit up and winced in pain. "Could have been worse. At least I'm still breathing."

"Want to tell me what happened?"

"I was headed here to make my Sunday rounds. When the light changed at Main, I hit the brakes, but nothing happened. Damned pedal went all the way to the floor. I grabbed the emergency brake, but it was too late."

The skin around his left eye was puffed and dark, and someone had stitched the peak of his left eyebrow. If the Bronco had been going a few miles faster, I'd have another name to add to my list of clinic fatalities. "Brake failure?"

"Couldn't have been. My car's almost new. Just had it in for its three-thousand-mile checkup. Somebody must have tampered with them."

"Don't you keep your car locked in your garage overnight?"

"I gave my daughter a Ping-Pong table for her birthday a few weeks ago. It's set up in the garage, so there's only room for Stephanie's car. Mine stays in the driveway. Anybody could've had access to it."

Aware of doctors and nurses bustling in and out of the adjoining cubicles, I leaned toward him and lowered my voice. "I know you're in debt up to your eyeballs. You owe anybody money who might resort to drastic collection techniques?"

"I may be foolish enough to run up debts, but I know enough to stay away from the tough guys." He shook his head, grimaced with pain and lay still. "I joined Gamblers Anonymous, and I'm slowly knocking down my bills. It'll take a while, but I'm determined. I owe it to my wife and kids."

"A man like you must carry a lot of insurance. Enough to clear your debts and leave a comfortable sum for your family?"

His eyes narrowed. "I'm no coward, Detective. Suicide would be the gutless way out."

"Where did you go when you left the country club yesterday?"

"Straight home. And my brakes worked fine then. I didn't leave the house until this morning."

If I'd placed Bill on surveillance sooner, he might have caught whoever had played havoc with Tillett's brakes. For now, I was left with only speculation. Tillett had some speculations of his own.

"You think whoever did this is the same person who killed Castleberry and the others?"

"I intend to find out."

Chaos erupted in the trauma section as a new patient was wheeled in. The patient's screams, doctors shouting instructions to nurses, and the cloying, coppery smell of blood filled the air.

Tillett's blue eyes locked gazes with mine. "You and I are a lot alike. I deal with illnesses and injuries that affect the body. You struggle against the diseases of society, crime that festers like a wound and sometimes kills. Either way, we both encounter more death, destruction and sorrow than any human being should have to witness and still be able to sleep at night."

The new patient continued to scream in the cubicle at the end of the room.

"I gambled to escape," Tillett said. "How do you block out the sights and sounds of so much misery?"

Stephanie Tillett's arrival spared me from answering. I left the Tilletts and averted my eyes from the battered body surrounded by a trauma team at the other end of the room.

I drove straight to the parking lot of Sophia's, where Adler was tailing Morelli and Dorman, apprised Adler of Tillett's accident, and told him to take the rest of the day off. That day and evening I watched for Dorman and entertained myself trying to distinguish tourists from residents among the crowds that strolled the marina docks and frequented the restaurants.

A little after midnight, Dorman exited the restaurant, supporting Morelli, who staggered from drink. Dorman helped the big man into the front seat of Dorman's ancient Buick and drove away.

I followed them to the entrance to Pelican Point and waited while Dorman drove his boss to his house and helped him inside. Dorman then drove to his garage apartment and didn't leave until early the next morning when he went straight to the Body Shop on U.S. 19.

Lucky for me, a Dunkin' Donuts shared the gym's parking lot. I was refueling on leaded coffee and a cruller when my beeper squawked. At a pay phone in the parking lot, I called Bill and watched for Dorman to leave the gym.

"Someone drained the brake fluid from Tillett's car, all right," Bill said. "There's a puddle of it in his driveway. You can have a tech check the car for prints, but anyone who'd go to this kind of trouble probably used gloves."

"Nothing to indicate whether Tillett might have done it himself?"

"Sorry, a dead end there. What's next?"

"Nothing until tonight. I'll need you to keep an eye

on Dorman while I have dinner with the Queen Mother at the yacht club."

Dorman came out of the gym and hopped into his car. I put on my sunglasses and strolled toward my Volvo. He didn't glance my way as he pulled onto the highway.

When I trailed him into town past City Hall, a crowd of senior citizens thronged the sidewalks, carrying posters and chanting, "Keep our police department." I didn't see any proponents for the other side. Councilman Ulrich had stirred up a hornet's nest with his cost-cutting proposal.

Dorman reported for work at the restaurant, and I settled in for a long wait, thankful it was October and not July. With the windows down and a sea breeze blowing through, the interior of the Volvo was tolerable in the unshaded lot. I took out my grid of suspects and searched for a missing link, something to make sense of all the disjointed and seemingly purposeless events. Nothing clicked.

Twice during the day, I walked across to use the park restroom and the pay phone at the marina. I talked with Marilee Ginsberg, Rosco Fields and Charlene Jamison, the remaining patients in Karen's group at the clinic, but none had noted anything suspicious in the last few days. I warned them to be cautious and wished I had the manpower to offer some protection. The only real safeguard I could give them would be catching the killer before he could strike again.

At six o'clock, Bill moved his car from his reserved space by the docks and pulled up beside me. I waved and mouthed thanks and hurried home to shower and dress for dinner.

I abandoned the calamine and Benadryl creams, took extra care with my makeup and put on a new pair of black slacks with a burgundy blouse, slate-gray blazer and low-heeled pumps. I appraised myself in the mirror. For an aging old broad, I cleaned up pretty good.

Mother almost gushed when I met her and Cedric Langford in the club lobby. "Margaret, I'd almost forgotten what a beautiful woman you can be."

As she inclined her cheek for a kiss, she whispered in my ear, "Cedric will be impressed."

I doubted Cedric would notice. He was too busy eyeing the buns of steel of a young waiter carrying a tray of drinks from the adjoining bar to the dining room.

When Caroline and Hunt joined us, we moved to our table in the dining room. I'd learned my lesson from the week before and had given up Benadryl capsules for the day. To keep a clear head, I ordered a club soda with a twist of lime. As sleep-deprived as I was, even a whiff of alcohol would have sent me into a deep coma.

My brother-in-law almost managed what I'd attempted to avoid. His long, droning account of his latest group-policy sale to a large software company in Pinellas Park had all of us drowsing, until Cedric picked up the pace during the main course with a lively account of Prince Charles's recent visit with the polo set in Fort Lauderdale.

After Mother's initial effusiveness, she lapsed into silence. I grew concerned when she declined dessert. "Are you all right, Mother?"

She smiled weakly. "Just a little tired. I'm not as young as I used to be. Perhaps, Caroline, you and Hunt could drive me home now."

Caroline sprang to her feet and Hunt hovered over Mother, supporting her on a beefy arm when she rose from her chair.

My initial alarm dissipated with the conspiratorial smile Mother threw me as they left me alone with Cedric. Her health and her matchmaking were in tiptop shape.

I waited until she'd left the room before I turned to

Cedric. "Sorry to back out on you, but I'm in the middle of a murder investigation."

He stood, pulled out my chair and offered his hand. "Good luck, Detective." His attention drifted to the waiter at the next table.

I followed his glance. "Happy hunting to you, too."

His gray eyes glittered with amusement as he realized he hadn't fooled me. He was a nice guy, but definitely not what Mother had in mind for a son-in-law.

I strode through the lobby, out the double front doors, and straight into a robbery in progress. Hunt's Lincoln Town Car stood beneath the portico with the driver's door wide open. A young black male had backed the teenage valet against the hood with a gun at his back. Another teenager had his arm around Mother's throat in a chokehold and a small pistol rammed against her temple. Hunt and Caroline stood frozen beside her.

I drew my weapon and yelled, "Police! Drop your guns!"

The youth holding the valet wavered. He looked about thirteen and as scared as his captive was. But the kid clutching Mother was older, maybe fifteen, with a dead, blank expression that frightened me. He had the cold look of a killer, one who would steal what he wanted, then shoot for the fun of it.

"Back off, bitch," the older boy yelled at me, "or the old lady's history."

"That old lady is my mother, you rotten little bastard, and if you touch that trigger, I'll blow your fucking brains out."

His grip tightened on Mother's throat. "You can't get us both. You shoot me and my man over there will nail you."

The kid he called his man looked ready to wet his pants.

"Don't count on it," I said. "I'm fast and I'm accurate. And the Black Talons in this gun will rip you apart. With those peashooters you're carrying, you'd barely scratch me, even if you could fire off a round before I kill you."

The younger boy backed away from the valet, set his gun down and put his hands in the air. "I just wanted the money. Don't hurt me, lady."

The valet scooped up the gun, brought it to me, and I tucked it in the waistband of my slacks.

"Call 911," I told him.

My adrenaline was spiking. Mother no longer appeared imperious or overbearing, but a pitiful old woman at the mercy of a street punk. I'd have pulled the trigger gladly just to make him pay for the terror he was inflicting on her.

I watched his eyes as I inched forward and caught a flicker of hesitation. "Put the gun down now, before you find yourself in worse trouble."

While the yacht club yielded rich pickings for thieves, its location on the end of Pelican Beach, an island with only one causeway to the mainland, made getaways difficult. The sirens in the distance distracted him. With the patrol cars approaching, his only way out was to swim, and I'd bet my pay that this punk couldn't even dog-paddle.

He tossed his gun aside and released Mother. Hunt caught her as she almost fell.

"Down on your faces, both of you," I screamed at the youths. "Spread your arms and legs and keep your noses to the pavement."

I retrieved the other gun and stood guard over the skinny young bodies until the patrol cars arrived. Steve Johnson and Rudy Beaton cuffed the perps. While Steve took witness statements, Rudy corralled the hoodlums into the back of his cruiser. The youngest one was crying with deep, choking sobs, but the older boy scowled at me with a withering look.

Mother, pale and trembling, sat hunched on the back seat of the Town Car. Caroline sat beside her, holding her hand. Hunt looked green around the gills.

"Maybe you should have a doctor check you out, Mother," I said.

She straightened her back and a bit of her old starch returned. "I'm perfectly well. It will take more than a street urchin to finish me off. And Margaret—"

I waited, anticipating for once in my life a crumb of praise, so long in coming. "Yes, Mother?"

"Where did you learn such deplorable language?" she said with a disapproving shake of her head, then closed the door.

I longed for sleep as I stumbled toward the door of my condo, but the adrenaline still coursing through my body would keep me awake for a long time. I'd slipped my key into the lock, when a figure detached itself from the shadow of the golden rain tree by the entrance.

"Detective Skerritt?"

As hyper as I was, I had to exert all my control to keep from drawing my gun and drilling the person who'd scared the crap out of me.

A young woman stepped into the circle of illumina-

tion from the porch light, and I recognized Gale Whatley, Dr. Tillett's office manager.

"I have to talk with you," she said. "I've been waiting for hours."

It was late, but in the shape I was in, I wouldn't fall
asleep anytime soon. "Come on in."

She hesitated. "It's about the murders. I'm here to
make a confession."

CHAPTER 19

I switched on the lights and motioned Gale in ahead of me. With the collar of her coat turned up and her hands thrust deep in her pockets, she halted in the middle of the living room. Her eyes appeared out of focus, and when she removed her coat, her hands shook.

"Sit down." I took her coat and pointed to a deep rattan chair.

She perched on the edge of the seat, gripping the front of the cushion with her lacquered nails, like a wild animal ready to bolt at the first noise. When I'd first interviewed her, her looks and composure had reminded me of a fashion model on the runway. Tonight, in scruffy jeans and faded T-shirt with slipshod makeup and flyaway hair, she could have worked undercover vice with Lenny Jacobs, except that the nervous tremors racking her body would have given her away.

"I should have told you before." She kept her voice low and studied the carpet in front of her toes.

I eased my bone-weary body into a chair across from her and hoped my adrenaline high would keep me awake long enough to hear what she had to say.

She raised her hands, and her long fingers splayed across her throat, as if protecting it. "I wouldn't have come at all, except I visited Rich in—"

"Rich?"

"Dr. Tillett. I went to see him in the hospital. I told him you had to know."

I curbed my inclination to prod her. In the strained silence, the grandfather clock ticked loudly, and in the kitchen, the refrigerator motor kicked on with a whir.

"I'm sorry I lied to you," she blurted. "I didn't think it would harm anyone, but now..."

Tears glistened in her eyes, rolled across her high cheekbones and smeared her botched makeup. For all her veneer of sophistication, she was just a scared kid.

I reached across the pass-through counter into the kitchen for a box of tissues and handed it to her. "Why don't you start at the beginning?"

She plucked a tissue and wiped her eyes. "Rich didn't kill his patients. You have to believe that."

"He had a reason, a million-dollar reason. And he

has no alibis. That puts him right up at the top of my list of suspects."

She shook her head with such force, her dark hair fell forward, covering one eye. She pushed it back and glared at me. "But he does have an alibi. That's what I'm trying to tell you."

"For the night Peter Castleberry was murdered?"

"For all of them. He was with me." A flush darkened her fair complexion.

"How do I know you're not making this up to protect him?"

"I have the hotel receipt from the weekend in Boca Raton." She fumbled in her purse, withdrew a crumpled paper and handed me a credit card slip from the Marriott in Boca. "Rich came straight to my room after he checked in at the resort and stayed until the time for his meeting the next morning. And the night Peter died, Rich was at my house."

She seemed too embarrassed by her admissions to be lying. "You'd have made my job a lot easier if you'd told me this in the first place."

Fresh tears welled in her eyes. "I couldn't. We were afraid Stephanie would find out."

I nodded with fake sympathy. "A wife can be such an inconvenience at times like these."

"That's not the way it was." She raised her chin in defiance. "Rich loves her. His family means more to him than anything."

This was definitely a different twist from the old my-wife-doesn't-understand-me excuse. "Pardon my silly question, but if he's so crazy about his wife, why is he having an affair with you? And vice versa."

"It all started with the gambling. When Stephanie learned how much money Rich had lost and the size of the debt he'd accumulated, she was furious. If it hadn't been for the children, she'd have walked out. The threat of losing her brought him to his senses. That's when he joined Gamblers Anonymous, but breaking his addiction was tough, and Stephanie wouldn't speak to him, much less help him."

"And you decided to play Florence Nightingale?"

"I do the bookkeeping, so I knew about the debt. Rich needed emotional support, someone to cheer him on in his struggle to regain control of his life, and he wasn't getting it from Stephanie."

I refrained from commenting that support probably wasn't all he wasn't getting from Stephanie. "So your adultery is just a higher form of altruism?"

Sarcasm laced my voice, and she winced at its bite.

"I know it looks bad, but I wasn't trying to be a home wrecker. I've known all along, when this is all over, Rich will go back to Stephanie. That's why I couldn't tell you. If she found out about me, she might never love him again."

I studied the tearstained face, wondering if masochism was gender-specific. I'd met too many women who'd ruined their lives loving the wrong man. "Why tell me all this now?"

"Because Rich's life is in danger. Whoever killed his patients is trying to kill him. You have to believe me. You have to protect him."

I believed her. Such a pathetic story would be hard to make up. She wanted me to save him to live happily ever after with his wife and children. I couldn't decide whether the woman was an idiot or a saint.

After Gale left, I slept for a few hours before reporting for work, but stakeout is not the most stimulating activity. I'd almost dozed off midmorning when Adler tapped on my car window. He slid onto the front seat of my Volvo, parked at the rear of the lot at Sophia's, where I had a clear view of all entrances and exits.

"I checked the serial number on the .22 you found

at Englewood's," he said. "It's the same gun stolen from that old couple the night Edith Wainwright was killed."

"Ballistics report back yet?"

"Nope, but the lab matched the tear on the duct tape on its barrel with the duct tape on the plastic bottle Castleberry's shooter used as a silencer. Guess that confirms our killer is a man."

"How do you figure?"

"The couple whose house was robbed the night Wainwright died, the thief was a man."

"Maybe the thief fenced the gun or sold it on the street. There's big money in stolen weapons."

"Before I forget—" he dug into the pocket of his leather jacket and handed me a letter "—this came for you at the station."

I slit open the pale blue envelope to find a typed letter from Anastasia Gianakis that read, "I'm sorry to have missed you on Saturday. Please call me at your EARLIEST convenience. I must talk with you about the circumstances of my niece's death."

Something bothered me about the letter, and I stared at it for a moment before the detail registered.

I shoved the paper into Adler's hand. "Take this back to the station. Look in the evidence room for a white card with Karen Englewood's name typed on it and send them both to the lab."

"What's up?" he asked.

"Check out the word *earliest*, typed in capitals. There's a broken serif on the E, just like on the card I found at Edith's house. If the typewriters are a match, it puts Anastasia at the scene of the crime." I opened my door and climbed out of the car. "I'll ask Bill to take over here, then I'm going to pay our typist a visit."

I negotiated a gauntlet of cats, sleeping in the morning sun on Anastasia's front porch, and rang the bell. Like the other houses on the narrow, winding street, Anastasia's looked like something from the Greek islands with its glistening white paint, Mediterranean-blue trim and bright fall flowers that bordered her front walk.

When she opened her door, the pungent smell of garlic and cinnamon escaped. She wiped her hands on a white apron and smoothed the severe lines of her black dress over her plump curves. Eyes like chunks of obsidian squinted at me in the bright sunlight.

I displayed my badge and introduced myself. "I'm here in response to your letter."

Her squint dissolved into a warm smile that revealed traces of the beauty the Gianakis brothers had fallen in love with. She swung open the screen door and led me into a front room cluttered with overstuffed furniture. "Sit down. I'll fix some coffee."

Before I could decline, she hurried away down a dark hallway and left me alone with a gigantic chinchilla Persian draped across the back of the sofa like a feather boa. A round table at the sofa's end displayed photographs in silver frames, most of them of a dark-haired man and a stunning girl with shining black eyes, Vasily and Anastasia in their youth.

In one corner, burning tapers flanked two gilded icons of saints, painted in Byzantine style in bright primary colors. The heavy scent of sandalwood from a brass incense burner permeated the air. A massive Remington typewriter dominated a desk in the opposite corner.

In a few minutes Anastasia returned with a loaded tray and served thick Turkish coffee in small cups and tiny cookies she called *koulourakia*.

Before I discussed her letter, I had a few other items that needed clearing up. "When you spoke to Officer Adler, you told him you didn't know Edith Wainwright, but Peter Castleberry said you personally delivered a cat to her house."

"Your young man did not ask if I had ever met the

poor girl. He asked if I knew her. To meet and to know are different things." She smiled as if I were a backward child to whom she was kind enough to explain the obvious.

"Last Friday night, when Castleberry was killed, where were you?"

"I went to special services at the church. The good father can vouch for me."

"You're using God as your alibi?"

Her black eyes crinkled with laughter. "Not God, although he saw me, too. Father Theo, my priest."

I made a note to check with the Orthodox priest on my way out of Tarpon. "Now, this letter you sent me—"

"You are going to arrest him, yes?"

"Him?"

"Lester Morelli, the monster who killed poor little Sophia."

"I can't arrest him. There's no evidence."

"What about the evidence from Sophia's own lips. She told me he was mistreating her. She was going to the islands to get away from him." She dunked a cookie in her coffee, popped it into her mouth and crunched with a fierceness probably intended for Morelli.

"I have at least a dozen people," I said, "who claim

otherwise, people with nothing to gain from having Morelli indicted."

"Humph. If you do not believe me, then why are you here?"

"To ask about your typewriter." I nodded toward the Remington.

She set down her cup and extended her hands toward me to expose misshapen fingers and swollen joints. "My arthritis is so bad, I can no longer hold the pen. The last day I saw her, Sophia gave me the typewriter so I can write to my family in Greece."

"It came from Sophia's house?"

"No, no." She shook her head. "It came from the restaurant. Sophia had Antonio deliver it to her house when she knew I was coming. Since she was disposing of it, anyway, she gave it to me."

"Why did she get rid of it?"

"The chef's assistant used to type the special entrée cards for the menus, but when Lester bought a new computer system with printers, they had no need for this."

"Who had access to the typewriter at the restaurant?"

"It was kept in the kitchen, so anyone who worked there could have used it. But why do you talk of typewriters when Lester Morelli is walking free?"

"Because your typewriter might be a link to the killer, Mrs. Gianakis."

"You must arrest this man, Detective, so my sweet Sophia can rest in peace."

Anastasia could have typed the card I'd found by Edith's door, but it didn't feel right. I didn't scratch her completely off my list. Ted Bundy, Florida's most notorious serial killer, had been famous for his charm, and too many had died as a result of it.

The priest confirmed Anastasia's alibi.

For almost a week after my visit with her, Bill, Adler and I concentrated on Dorman and Morelli and kept track of every move they made. Both had had access to the typewriter that had printed Karen's name on the gift card found at Edith's house. I waited for one of them to incriminate himself.

Morelli simply continued to drink himself into a stupor. Every night, either Dorman or Antonio drove a polluted Lester home, then brought him back to the restaurant the next morning. Adler and I placed bets on which would last longer, Morelli's grief or his liver.

Dorman was an obsessive-compulsive who never varied his routine. He jogged on the trail at sunrise, worked out at the Body Shop, then reported in time to work the luncheon crowd at the restaurant. He drove straight home at night, with the exception of occasional escort duty for his intoxicated boss.

Chief Shelton stayed on my back and pressed for a solution for the case. The debate over disbanding the department had divided the citizens of Pelican Bay into two angry camps. More than eight thousand had signed petitions to keep the force intact, while another local group, hoping for tax relief if the sheriff's department took over, was slowly growing in numbers. The longer the diet-clinic murders went unsolved, the worse it looked for the home team.

The first homicide had occurred three weeks ago, and we had no arrests to show for it. The delay had done nothing to improve my disposition or my skin condition. I sat in the darkness in the Volvo, scratching and watching the Friday night crowds enter and leave the restaurant. After learning about the typewriter, which the lab had matched to the card found at Edith's, I felt certain either Dorman or Morelli was my man, but I needed more than the feeling in my gut to make charges stick.

Meanwhile, I couldn't take a chance that the killer might strike again, so neither Morelli nor Dorman drew a breath that I didn't know about.

At ten-thirty, Adler's car pulled next to mine, and he joined me in my car. "You expecting the same routine tonight?"

I nodded. "Which do you want when they leave, Dorman or Morelli?"

He unwrapped a stick of gum and poked it in his mouth. "Doesn't make much differ—"

"Look." I grabbed his arm. "I think this week of terminal boredom's about to pay off."

As the restaurant's side door, marked Private, opened and closed, dim light briefly silhouetted a man's body. The figure slipped through the shadows to the back of Morelli's Mercedes, parked in its reserved spot, and opened the trunk. The interior light illuminated his face as he shoved something in his belt and withdrew a small package. He closed the lid softly and headed for the marina park in a nonchalant walk.

"It's Morelli," Adler said.

"Yeah, and if that's the walk of a drunk, I'm Miss America." I opened my door. "Let's go. The missing piece of our puzzle just fell into place."

CHAPTER 20

Morelli sauntered into the park like a man with no specific destination. He circled the bandstand, stopped at the water fountain for a drink, then continued south. Adler and I followed at a distance.

When Morelli exited the park onto the jogging path that paralleled Edgewater, we lengthened the space between us and him. Without the cover of deep shadows from the park's trees, we risked being recognized if we came too close.

I grabbed Adler's hand and laced my fingers through his. When he tried to jerk away, I tightened my grip and whispered, "Hold my hand, dammit. If he looks back, I want him to see lovers on a moonlight stroll. I don't want to spook him."

"You're spooking me," Adler muttered.

For several blocks we ambled behind Morelli, who paused only once to look back. A block later, with his package tucked under his arm, he stopped to light a cigarette.

I stopped, too, and threw my arms around Adler's neck. "Hug me," I whispered, "but don't take your eyes off him. We'll break off when he starts to move away."

"Jesus, Maggie, I feel like I'm seducing my own mother."

"You'd be rotten at undercover, Adler," I whispered in his ear. "You have no imagination."

Morelli took his time with his cigarette. I kept my face pressed against the soft leather of Adler's jacket. "What's he doing now?"

"He just flicked the butt into the bay. He's moving on." Adler released me.

"Not yet." I tightened my hold on his neck. "Give it a minute."

"Hell, Maggie, you act like you're enjoying this." He squirmed.

"And if you don't act that way, too, you'll blow our cover." I waited another moment, then dropped my arms. "Let's move."

"Thank God." Adler stepped away, jerked his jacket over his hips and fell into step beside me. "Where do you think he's headed?"

"If I'm right, you'll see for yourself in a few seconds."

Morelli fulfilled my expectations by leaving the path, crossing Edgewater and strolling up Windward Lane toward Karen Englewood's house.

Adler and I sprinted past Windward to the next block and raced through the yard of the house behind Karen's. We crept across her backyard, up the drive, and hid in the shadow of the tall pittosporum hedge that edged her front porch.

The house was dark, and the ringing door chimes carried through the open windows. Upstairs, a door opened, footsteps pattered down the staircase, and the porch light came on.

I withdrew deeper into the hedge when the front door lock clicked, and Karen's voice floated out into the night. "Lester? What are you doing here?"

"I'm sorry to bother you so late, but I had to see you." Lester's voice oozed sincerity.

"Why?" Karen sounded half asleep. He'd probably awakened her.

"Grief," he said. "It's driving me crazy. I've been drinking too much, trying not to think about how much I miss Sophia. Then I realized the only way out of this pain is to stop pitying myself and to think of others instead. I won't take long. I've brought you something."

Karen hesitated, then the door swung wider. "Sure, come in."

Footsteps sounded and the front door closed. "Watch the back door," I whispered to Adler.

He slipped away into the darkness, and I advanced up the porch steps, keeping out of the line of sight from the living room windows where the lights had come on and the shadows of Karen and Morelli were outlined on the draperies.

The front door was unlocked. I eased it open and crept into the foyer. Through the broad arch that led into the living room, I could see the back of the chair where Karen sat, but Morelli was off to the side, out of sight.

"You were so kind," he said. "Sophia owed her progress entirely to you. I brought you a small present to show my gratitude."

I hoped I'd figured right. Morelli sounded so sincere, he almost had me believing him. If his late-night jaunt proved no more sinister than a grateful gesture, Shelton would have my head for illegal entry, and the department, whose survival already looked tenuous, would suffer.

"A gift isn't necessary," Karen said. "I liked Sophia and was happy to help her."

"But I want you to have it. I hope you like chocolate."

Chocolate.

Edith Wainwright's stomach had held traces of chocolate along with the cyanide. I pulled my gun and started to move, then hesitated at Karen's next words.

"I love chocolate, but not at night. The caffeine in it keeps me awake."

"Please—" his seductive voice enticed her "—just one, so I'll know you like them."

"I do appreciate your gift, but—"

"Just one, and then I'll leave."

"All right, but chocolates are like potato chips with me. It's hard to stop once I've started."

I stepped into the room.

Morelli's eyes widened and flickered with annoyance before he smiled. "Detective Skerritt, how nice to see you. Why the gun?"

Karen sat stunned, holding the box of chocolates.

I moved toward her. "Don't touch those, Karen. And you, Morelli. Put your hands up and back away."

He shrugged, lifted his hands and smiled again, a charming psychopath. But when Karen leaned forward to place the box of chocolates on the coffee table, Morelli jerked a handgun from his belt with one hand and, with the other, yanked Karen in front of him like a shield.

"It's no use," I said. "My partner's out back. All I have to do is call him."

Morelli rammed the barrel of the gun against Karen's temple. "Don't. Put down your gun and let me go, or I'll kill her."

"And once she's dead, what then?" I raised the volume of my voice, hoping Adler would hear. "You'll kill me and then my partner? You kill a cop, and every law-enforcement officer in the country will be after your hide. You've botched this one, Morelli. Let her go and give yourself up."

"Not until she pays for all the trouble she's caused. If it wasn't for this meddling bitch, Sophia would have died years ago and saved me all this trouble." He pulled Karen tighter against him. His hand covered her mouth and nose, and she was struggling to breathe, but I couldn't get a straight shot at Morelli with her in the way.

I had to play for time for Adler to get into position. "Why Edith, Peter and Tillett?"

His grin was chilling. "Edith was to throw suspicion off me. I couldn't have Sophia the only victim. But you didn't have a clue what was happening. And I found

PELICAN BAY

out I *liked* killing. I was good at it. It was a game where I always came out the winner. So while I was at it, I took my revenge on the whole damned clinic that kept Sophia alive too damned long, and pinned the blame on Karen here."

A shadow moved in the dining room and worked its way behind Morelli. At first, I thought it was Adler. The man moved like a flash, arms flexed, a baseball bat in his hands. Before anyone else knew he was there, he clobbered Morelli with a two-handed swing, laying him out cold on the living room floor. Morelli's gun skittered across the hardwood surface.

"You all right, Mom?" Larry dropped the bat and led his shaken mother to a chair.

Adler had entered on Larry's heels and knelt beside Morelli. He felt for a pulse, then snapped his cuffs on the unconscious man's wrists. "He's still breathing. I'll call an ambulance."

"Phone's in the office." Larry jerked his head toward the room across the hall, and Adler sprinted out of the room.

"So you decided to come home after all?" I said to Larry.

"Moved back yesterday, and a good thing, too." He scowled at Morelli's still form and draped an arm around his mother's shoulders. "Mom and I worked things out."

He'd cut his hair, and his eyes were clear, drug-free.

Karen averted her gaze from the man stretched out on her Aubusson rug and squeezed Larry's hand on her shoulder. "Larry has a new job."

While we waited for the ambulance, I patted down Morelli's pockets and extracted two envelopes, one containing potassium ferricyanide crystals, the other, a typed suicide note in Karen's name, claiming she'd killed Edith, Sophia, Peter and Tillett because her work at the clinic had wrecked her marriage. Because she couldn't live with her guilt, the note said, she was taking her own life.

Morelli had thought of almost everything. Across the hallway in her study, a typewriter sat on the credenza behind her desk. I slipped in a clean sheet and typed a few words. The fonts matched. When the lab checked the note, they'd probably confirm it had been typed on Karen's machine. As cool as Morelli had been, he'd most likely written it during the break-in when he'd planted the gun that had killed Castleberry in her desk. He hadn't known then that Tillett would survive his car accident.

"How could he do it?" Karen asked as the paramedics wheeled Morelli out.

I shrugged. "A killer's mind is a strange and twisted thing. Like he said, at first to cover his tracks, then as a game he enjoyed winning, the ultimate experience in power and control. And with the note he'd planned to leave on your body, he'd have his scapegoat and clear access to Sophia's fortune at last."

"But," Larry said, "he didn't get away with it, thanks to you."

I grinned at him. "You did all right yourself."

The *Ten-Ninety-Eight*, held fast by its anchor, bobbed in the clear turquoise waters off Caladesi Island. Bill and I had just finished a picnic breakfast on the beach. I tugged the hem of my bathing suit where it had crept over my butt and reached for my beach bag.

"This is the life," I said. "Gorgeous November weather, a beach all to ourselves and four more days of vacation, sans beeper." I sat cross-legged on the blanket and rubbed lotion on my arms and legs.

"More hives?" Bill asked. "I thought those cleared up after the grand jury indicted Morelli."

"They did. This is sunscreen."

Bill stretched out on his back with his arms folded behind his head and eyed me over the rim of his sunglasses. "You have to admit, the guy almost got away with it."

I spread a blob of sunscreen across my nose and cheeks. "His alibis threw us. By the time he killed

Edith, he'd already established the precedent of locking himself in his office on Fridays to do his bookkeeping. Then after Sophia's murder, he locked himself in every night with a full bottle of whiskey, which he probably splashed on his clothes, then poured the rest down the drain. Acting so drunk his staff had to drive him home was a convincing touch."

"You'd never have caught him without surveillance."

"You're right. All Morelli had to do was waltz out his side door. He was within walking distance of Edith's, the trail and Karen Englewood's. His car never left its reserved spot. We found a roll of duct tape in the trunk. The tear matches the tape on the homemade silencer. Rags with brake fluid matching the brand used in Tillett's Infiniti were also in his trunk. And as glib as Morelli is, he can't explain away his confession in front of Karen and me."

Bill shook his head. "I'd have thought he was too smart to incriminate himself."

"Pride overrode his common sense and did him in. He had to brag about his accomplishments."

"He must have planned everything for months."

"Six, at least. That's when he stole the cyanide from Castleberry." I squirted sunscreen on Bill's bare chest. "He married Sophia only because he knew she was dying, hoping in a matter of a few years to have all her money and no ball and chain. A trained actor, he played the devoted husband and waited. Then Karen and Dr. Tillett appeared on the scene and restored Sophia to health. Frustrated the hell out of Morelli, who'd planned to claim his inheritance within a couple of years and run. Sophia could have lived a long life once she brought her weight and diabetes under control, so he was forced to take drastic action."

"Then the old woman was right?"

"Sophia had confided to Anastasia that her marriage was on the rocks, but Morelli used the Gianakis family feud to his advantage, turning any accusations the aunt made against him back onto her. The aunt's testimony helped convince the grand jury. She brought letters Sophia had written to cousins in Greece that arrived weeks after her funeral. They expressed her desire for a divorce, her intention to change her will, and her fear that Lester might harm her before she could leave the country."

Anastasia had inherited Sophia's estate. She had put the restaurant and resort on the market and planned to use the proceeds for a shelter for stray cats.

"We couldn't have caught Morelli without your help," I said. "I wonder if there's any way to make

Councilman Ulrich understand the importance of adequate manpower."

"Don't you mean personpower, O Liberated One?" Bill scooped a blob of lotion off his chest and flicked it at me.

I snorted in what my mother would have termed a very unladylike way. "I can't worry about semantics. Liberated is as liberated does."

He sat up and grabbed my hands, still slick with sunscreen. "How about liberating yourself from this job? If you insist on working, we can form our own private detective agency, call our own shots."

"Skerritt and Malcolm?"

"Hmm, S & M. It has a certain ring to it. Even better, how about M & M, Malcolm and Malcolm. Marry me."

I was convinced he was joking, as usual. I could solve murders, but had yet to learn to put together the pieces of my personal life. I shook my head and grinned. "I have just the ticket to cure you of any matrimonial ambitions toward me."

"What?"

"Thanksgiving's next week. The Queen Mother is having dinner catered at her house. Why not join us?"

"Ah, Margaret." He put his arms around me. "Finally

taking me home to meet the family. You may end up married to me yet."

"Once you meet my mother, trust me, you'll change your mind."

"I've been after you for almost twenty years. What makes you think I'd give up now?"

Twenty years? Now I was sure he was teasing, and I couldn't help myself. He'd set me up. "Old age?"

I jogged down to the breakers to wash off the sand he'd tossed on me.

Bill followed. "Be serious, Margaret. We'd make a great P.I. team."

"And spend the rest of my life tracking down errant husbands and cheating wives? No, thanks."

"Then at least promise you'll retire from the department."

"No promises, except one." I put my arms around his neck and kissed him. "You'll always be my best friend."

He leaned back and grinned.

"What are you smiling at?" I asked.

"Best friends. You'll find yourself married to me yet, Skerritt."

"Don't hold your breath, Malcolm. I'm an avowed spinster, set in my ways."

His grin widened and his blue eyes twinkled. "I love a challenge."

"You want a challenge? Last one in the water buys dinner tonight."

I scrambled to my feet and ran through the soft sand toward the water's edge. Bill caught up with me, grabbed me around the waist and kissed me.

"I'm not giving up, Maggie."

Shaken by the determination in his voice, I cupped his face in my hands. "Good," I said, and kissed him back.

* * * * *

Look for the next Maggie Skerritt mystery,
HOLIDAYS ARE MURDER,
coming in December 2005 only from
Charlotte Douglas and Harlequin NEXT.

REQUEST YOUR FREE BOOKS!

2 FREE NOVELS TO INTRODUCE YOU TO OUR BRAND-NEW LINE!

There's the life you planned. And there's what comes next.

HARLEQUIN®
Next™

Coming this September

With divorce and the big Four-Oh looming on the horizon, interior designer Kate Hennesy takes a step back to assess her life. Is it time to redecorate?

OUT WITH THE OLD, IN WITH THE NEW
From 2002 Golden Heart winner
Nancy Robards Thomson

HARLEQUIN®
Next™

COME OCTOBER

by *USA TODAY* bestselling author Patricia Kay

Victim of a devastating car accident, Claire Sherman couldn't bring herself to face the perfect fiancé and perfect life she'd lost. Starting over with a brand-new identity seemed like the best way to heal—but was it?

Available this October